Return of the
CRIMSON HOWL

Airship 27 Productions

TM

Return of the Crimson Howl
©2023 Paul Landri and Jason Clark

An Airship 27 Production
www.airship27.com
www.airship27hangar.com

Cover Illustration ©2023 Ted Hammond
interior illustrations ©2023 Sam Salas

Editor: Ron Fortier
Associate Editor: Rob Davis
Marketing and promotion: Michael Vance
Production designer Rob Davis.

ISBN: 978-1-953589-58-3

Printed in the United States of America

10 9 8 7 6 5 4 3 2 1

Return of the CRIMSON HOWL

by Paul Landri and Jason Clark

CHAPTER ONE

Benjamin Mulcahey walked around the desk where the body lay slumped over. The man's right abdomen had a large chunk missing and his severed intestines dripped brown fecal matter onto the Persian rug.

"I'll never get used to that smell," said Rourke.

They'd already sent away the three cops that were first on the scene. Between now and the time Forensics came, they could get down to business.

"Aye, because you shit roses and cinnamon buns," Ben said. His brogue echoed slightly in the large room. He pulled out a pair of latex gloves.

"So, who is this guy?" Rourke asked.

"I'd love to tell you, but we no longer have access to the who's who files. All we have is a buzzer that goes off when something strange happens near one of our VIPs." Ben took out a small flashlight and shined it on the man's face. He was a middle-aged African-American man. No different than anyone they had passed on the street earlier that day, except for the leaky sausage casing that was his intestines. His eyes were glazed over and his face was twisted in pain and horror.

"Hmm," Ben said. He stepped over to the other side of the body.

"Hmm?" Rourke echoed. "What do you mean, hmm?"

"I mean, hmm. Shut up and let me work."

Rourke shook his head. "Fine, fine. You're the expert."

"Be wise of you not to forget it," Ben smirked.

"Just ID the man already." Rourke sighed.

"To answer your question, old friend, this poor devil is none other than Doctor Parker J. McCoy."

Rourke shot Ben a puzzled look. "Who's Parker McCoy and how does this relate to the Golden Age?"

Ben turned his head away from the gore, took a deep breath, and began. "Historians place Parker McCoy as the godfather of the Golden Age. He graduated from Moorehouse College with a double doctorate in chemical and mechanical engineering. He was the guy most of the Exceptionals went to when they needed weapons or technology. Of course, it came with a pretty hefty price tag especially when it came to some of his serums."

"You're kidding me," Rourke scanned the room. "A black man was the mastermind behind the Exceptionals? Why'd I never hear about this?"

Ben looked up at Rourke, deadpan. "Because a black man was the mastermind behind the Exceptionals. Come on Rourke, how many people graded you better on tests than me, even though I was feeding you the answers."

Ben walked past the desk shining his flashlight on the framed items on the wall. Newspaper clippings about Golden Age heroes, civic and science awards, and photos of men and women in costumes, masks, and capes adorned them.

Rourke had taken out a camera and began to take pictures of the corpse.

"You say he was the godfather of the Golden Age but he looks pretty fresh. Like a man in his early fifties. He could be your father," Rourke snapped a photo of McCoy's face.

"There were rumors he had invented several chemical compounds to give regular people Exceptional abilities. It was claimed he found a way to slow the aging process. It's entirely possible those rumors were true," Ben said. "I certainly wouldn't be surprised. The man was considered a genius."

"Too bad he didn't invent a formula for being less tasty. Or, you know, some kind of anticannibal spray?" Rourke chuckled. "God, I'm funny."

Ben went back over to McCoy and inspected the gaping wound. "Look at these bite marks around the wound." He pointed to the periphery of the torn flesh.

"They don't look like human tooth marks, or teeth to me," Rourke said.

"Me either. Almost looks like an animal bite. A bear or maybe a lion." Ben shined his flashlight closer to the marks. "Look!"

"What?" Rourke moved in closer. "What is that?"

Ben turned to Rourke, "I can't believe it! They said he died back in the late 90's!"

Rourke tilted his head, "Who? What? What are you talking about?"

"I know it's a little hard to see, but look at the bite marks. Right there. Don't touch it!" Ben slapped at Rourke's hand.

"I wasn't going to!" Rourke said, "Will you tell me what got you so excited?"

"Those marks have mold on them! Which means he isn't dead after all."

"Wait. You don't mean..."

"I do. These bite marks are identical to the ones they found on fifteen different people back in the late 80s into the early 90s. The one thing they had in common, aside from the location, was the traces of black mold along the periphery of the wound."

"Fuck." Rourke exhaled a heavy sigh. "I think this is above our pay grade."

Rourke could almost see the gears in Ben's head turning.

"If this is what I think it is, Rourke, then it's going to be huge. Not just for you and I, but for our department."

Rourke would try to reason with Ben. He always tried. Never got him anywhere though. Typical Ben stubbornness, that. "The president said he was going to veto any spending on anything having to do with Golden Age preservation. You know it's something the politicians would like to forget despite everything Director Hollis has said."

Ben stood up. "When we came in the door to this study was open, yes?"

"Yes." Rourke concurred.

Rourke walked to the door and swung it closed. Scribbled on the wall behind the door in blood and shit were the words:

FIND
HOWL

"Fuck," Rourke said.

Ben walked over and clasped a hand on Rourke's shoulder. "Pack your bags, boyo. If Deacon James is killing again, we'd better get a move on. It's a long way to Los Angeles and he has a good head start."

CHAPTER TWO

It was an uneventful flight from Newark-Liberty Airport to LAX, save for a little turbulence over the Rocky Mountains.

Rourke alternated between dozing off and looking at the dossier Director Hollis had emailed him. He swiped through page after page of Golden Age history about the man formerly known as The Crimson Howl. Yawning between paragraphs, he would try to steal seconds of sleep, but Ben's persistent fidgeting fought him every step of the way.

Ben, of course, was wide awake and voraciously reading through every bit of the information. The Irishman grinned sharply.

"Can you please stop that?" Rourke said, "I know you're excited about this case but it's not like we're going to Disneyland."

"Are you kidding?" Ben's gray eyes were bright and fierce "This is better than some mouse in an amusement park, Rourke. We're going to meet the Crimson Howl himself!"

"Would you mind keeping it down? This is a classified mission after all. Why we're flying commercial is beyond me," Rourke cautioned.

Ben smiled. "No budget for our own plane."

"The least they could have done was to get us first-class tickets."

Ben went back to his tablet.

Rourke eventually followed suit. The names and faces of these costumed weirdos had become a blur to him over the years. It turned out this Howl guy that Ben was so excited about had been one of the first Exceptionals.

Though his place of birth was suspect, he'd gotten his start in Bayonne, New Jersey, roughing up street hoods in early 1940. His costume was a crimson shirt and pants, shiny, like something out of the circus with black trim near the elbows and down the pant legs. A gray wolf's head emblem is emblazoned on the chest. He wore a leather helmet that looked like something a bombardier from a war movie might wear, except it was lined with wolf fur and had pointed ears. He also had on a black mask covering his eyes and black and red gloves which, according to the files, had razor-sharp fingernails stitched into them.

Rourke decided he looked impossibly silly in the photo. Shit, most of these Golden Age yahoos seemed ludicrous. The costumes, with few exceptions, appeared to be dug up from a dollar store costume bin or worse. It was hard for him to imagine the appeal. Dressing up in a costume to beat up muggers? Why bother with having a police force at all if some joker in a mask and cape (which Rourke decided were even more pathetic than the actual costumes themselves) could beat someone half to death over a fucking misdemeanor? Very little of this so-called Golden Age made sense to Rourke. Of course, that, and Ben, were what drug him into investigating the period in the first place.

He was a detective first and the Golden Age was a problem to be solved. The idea galled him that there were people with powers who just stopped doing heroic things because Congress told them they weren't allowed to be vigilantes anymore. Who cared if there was a Federal law saying they couldn't don their outrageous outfits and fly around? There were people with the powers of gods out there and they let the President tell them they couldn't be heroes? Suddenly, they just hung up their capes, stupid-looking as they were, and went to work at Macy's? Why did the supervillains stop too? Neither side had needed permission to start brawling in the streets.

Rourke found that hardest to swallow. The villains were the only threats the Exceptionals were worth a damn at facing and they had just dried up and blown away. Ben had explained it to him once that when Congress outlawed Exceptional people from performing their heroics, the villains followed suit because it wasn't about crimes but the battle. With no heroes to fight, the villains just packed up and went home, too. Even the best therapy wasn't enough to cure most of them from a vicious cycle of larceny, rape, or murder. Why wouldn't it be the same for someone who could build a death ray?

"Ridiculous," Rourke muttered and kept reading.

The Crimson Howl, it was reported, was responsible for over 900 arrests from 1940 until 1971. He fought alongside Allied Forces in France in 1943 until the end of the war. His partner, an athletic fellow with a chiseled jaw and all-American good looks named Troy Berlin helped free over a hundred allied prisoners of war from a prison camp in Vichy. The Crimson Howl and the Human Bullet were thrown a parade in New York's Canyon of Heroes a month after V.E. Day.

Eventually, they would join forces with some of the more colorful members of the Golden Age to combat Communism. Sanctioned by Senator McCarthy, Howl and Troy Berlin teamed up with one Rudyard Sinclair, who called himself The Swami who claimed the source of his Exceptional abilities came from the medallion he wore around his neck. His powers had something to do with magic and mind manipulation, thus a guru getup complete with a tunic and Sikh turban.

Later, the three of them would meet up with Deacon James, a man who took no alias but had the oddest powers Rourke had ever heard of.

The stories claimed that Deacon James had been a janitor, just a few I.Q. points shy of being highly functional wallpaper. One night, a meteor fell from the sky and crashed through the Retreat Tower of the Brattleboro Asylum in Vermont where Deacon was mopping the linoleum. He went to investigate the damage, but when he came back out, the changes were drastic. Coworkers noticed that he spoke less than usual, which was good as far as they were concerned. What had been an overenthusiastic, jovial fool became solemn and detached. In this new mood, his most frequent companion for conversation was himself. The other employees began to complain anew about him having conversations with no one at all. He'd laugh unprovoked before immediately veering back to blank states.

Deacon would eventually leave the Brattleboro Asylum for unknown reasons. He would resurface a few months later assisting The Crimson Howl, The Human Bullet, and the Swami in fighting crime. As he fought beside them, his increased abilities became apparent and he left a residue of black mold behind as he passed.

When the Exceptional People's Act was repealed and crime-fighting became passé, the group disbanded and went their separate ways. The Human Bullet, because of his years of government service and the subject of genetic tests, was given a lifetime pension, health care, and a home for himself and his family.

Rudyard Sinclair seemingly vanished to parts unknown. Some say he went to Greece, others said he went wandering around the U.S. investigating strange occurrences under false names.

When the Elimination happened, rumors circulated that these former government strongmen were behind it, sanctioned by Nixon and the CIA.

Some believed it was part of Nixon's coverup of the Watergate Scandal. Others said he was attempting a political coup and would declare himself dictator of America and the only thing stopping him were Exceptional people. Rourke found this absurd. Surely the armed services would've stopped him. No need to assassinate heroes more suited to fistfights with ten story killbots than proper military engagements when so many others already stood in line to stop him.

After a period of quiet, as the bulk of the Exceptionals turned into a fresh layer of topsoil in their graveyard of choice, a new wave of Golden Age mania swept the states. The American Landscape in the early 1980's was rocked by a retro Golden Age explosion. The Crimson Howl released a tell-all book about his time working for McCarthy. Soon, one of the last remaining Golden Age heroes was everywhere.

He interviewed on the usual shows: Nightline with Ted Koppel and a two-hour-long special with Barbara Walters. Suddenly "Howl Fever" was everywhere. T-shirts and lunch boxes, toys and games, a cartoon by Hanna-Barbara, and a campy live-action TV show, which Rourke vaguely remembered liking as a kid, made the Crimson Howl a very rich man.

"Do you think the conspiracy theories are true?" Rourke asked. "You know, about the heroes who got murdered?"

Ben frowned, "I don't buy into conspiracy theories."

"But don't you find it odd that a bunch of people who happened to be Golden Age heroes, some with Exceptional abilities, were killed and there was never a direct cause? You don't think some supervillain hell-bent on revenge just straight-up murdered these people?" Rourke pressed.

"Historians agree the timing of the killings was strange, but it doesn't take into account the accidents, muggings, workplace mishaps and things like that." Ben looked up from his tablet.

"I'm not asking historians, I'm asking you. A ton of these vigilantes get picked off in numbers outdoing their active years, and we just write it off as normal day-to-day? Do you think Deacon James, who you and I both know from reading this stuff, had bizarre abilities, or had something to do with it? What about Howl? What about The Swami or The Human Bullet?"

"The Automatic Man," Ben added.

"What?"

Ben smiled. "Troy Berlin called himself The Automatic Man. It was his preferred alias but the papers liked The Human Bullet. It drove him crazy."

Rourke shook his head. "You're changing the subject. Do you think these guys had something to do with the killings in the Seventies?"

Ben sighed, "I suppose it's possible. I like to think it isn't true but I haven't researched it well enough to say one way or another. I do know that Deacon

James was responsible for non-powered murders in the early Seventies into the Nineties and that our buddies in the FBI tracked him down and shot him dead in a gazebo in a park in Brattleboro, Vermont." Ben paused. "My guess was he was trying to get back to where he found the meteor way back in the Forties."

"I guess they didn't do a good enough job giving him lead poisoning."

Ben smiled faintly. "His abilities may have had something to do with that or..."

Rourke raised his eyebrow. "Or?"

Ben's smile grew larger. "Or we're dealing with a copycat. Someone with similar powers. Maybe someone found the meteor, someone new. There's nothing in the files about where it wound up."

"Great," Rourke frowned. The thought of a potential second murderous man-beast on the loose sent a stiff chill up his spine.

CHAPTER THREE

Opulent was not a word Ben used in regular conversation. But here, it was appropriate. As they drove their little rented Nissan through the Beverly Hills streets Ben couldn't remember the last time he saw such expansive and elegant homes. The sidewalks were lined with lush, green palm trees and most of the homes had gates or fences to keep people out. A few of them had a little booth and a security guard stationed inside. Some had cars in the driveways that cost more than Ben had made since joining the Golden Age Task Force.

"Makes Parker McCoy's house look like a shanty," he commented.

"Honest to God, if we worked for the next hundred years we'd never be able to afford a sixth of what these houses are worth," Rourke agreed. "I'd go on about the fairness of it, but I don't want to get depressed."

Ben looked down at his smartphone. "Turn here, Lennox Drive."

Rourke turned onto a dead-end street. More palm trees lined the sidewalk. A small sign was posted a third of the way up the block: "Private Drive Ahead."

"You don't suppose the Crimson Howl owns all of this?" Rourke asked.

"When you're a celebrity, you can afford a little privacy, it seems," Ben replied. They reached the end of the street to what appeared to be a very long driveway.

"No gate," Rourke said. "That will make things easier. We can just knock on the door instead of using an intercom like a couple of jerk-offs."

They drove up the pristine black driveway, not knowing that it would be another half mile of palm trees and impeccably manicured lawn before they got up the hill and reached the estate of the Crimson Howl.

They were surprised to find the house was blocked off by a wrought iron gate. At the center was a silver wolf's head. Underneath in red were the letters C. H.

Rourke flashed a frustrated look at the intercom. "He owns the block leading up to his fucking property. He has a mile of driveway and the sonofabitch still has a gate? Either he's a tremendous asshole or he has a fucked-up sense of humor."

"You jinxed it, you horse's arse," Ben chuckled.

Rourke rolled down his window and stabbed his finger into the intercom buzzer. No answer. Rourke tried again. And again.

With a growl, Rourke opened his door and stepped out. He slammed it behind him and approached the gate.

Ben shouted after him from the car. "What are you doing?"

"Seeing if this stupid gate is locked." He went over to it and saw there was no padlock, just a latch keeping it closed. He lifted the latch and opened it. The gate was fairly heavy and required a bit of effort but it swung open. He got back into the car, slamming the door shut.

"I'm not sure I like this, Rourke. What if we're too late?"

"I didn't see any sign of that gate being forcibly opened. Something tells me he just isn't home. Or he's a dick."

Rourke came to a stop near the front of the house. A large fountain, which Rourke supposed was the centerpiece of the immaculately groomed and landscaped front lawn, was adorned with wolves, water falling from their mouths for infinity. Stone pillars ran from the ground all the way up to what appeared to be the third floor. Fifteen smooth bluestone steps separated the drive-way from the front door, which itself was painted crimson. A bronze knocker in the shape of a wolf's head. In its mouth was a bronze loop.

Rourke decided the whole thing looked painfully gaudy.

Ben's eyes were wide. "Holy shit!" He jumped out of the car and went up the bluestone steps. Rourke followed, shaking his head.

Ben knocked on the door and waited. Rourke caught up to him at the top of the steps.

"You think he heard you knock? This place is huge. What if he's in one of his fifty-eight bathrooms takin' a dump?" Rourke pushed the doorbell. A faint tune could be heard.

Ben smiled.

It was a chime version of the old Crimson Howl T.V. show theme.

They heard clunky footsteps coming down what sounded like wooden steps. A grunting bellow and finally, the snap of multiple locks being undone. The door opened only slightly.

"Fuck you want!?" A voice demanded. It was coarse and gruff. A voice of someone who spent a great deal of time drinking whiskey and smoking too many cigars. Hell, Rourke could smell the rich, peppery smoke of a cigar wafting from the crack in the door.

"Crimson Howl?" Ben queried.

"Who wants to know? You Mormons or a couple of them Scientology queers? I already told that sawed-off pipsqueak with that toothy shit-eating grin I ain't interested in gettin' my palm read or whatever the fuck they do."

Rourke produced his badge.

"Rourke Harken, Golden Age Task Force. My partner: Benjamin Mulcahey."

Ben produced his badge.

The door opened wider but not by much.

"Gimme those," said the growl.

The two agents obliged. The door closed. After a few moments, the door opened wide and the man finally showed himself. He was wearing red pajama pants, obviously, silk, and a stained A-shirt known or what Rourke knew as a "wife-beater" and a silk bathrobe white with black lotus flowers. His greasy hair was shoulder length, black with a streak or two of gray. He was wearing a pair of slippers that were dirty and scuffed. A cigar hung from the side of his mouth, as if it was contemplating escape. His face was lined and creased, his nose looked like it had been broken more than once and was beginning to show more than one gin blossom. Part of his left earlobe was missing and a scar traced a line from his right ear down his neck.

Despite this, he looked in decent shape with only a small pooch of a belly beginning to show. His mouth twisted into what Rourke assumed was a polite smile. He handed back their badges.

"Figured you guys were done for," he said.

"Beg pardon?" Ben asked.

"The Task Force. I figured they folded up." The Crimson Howl looked over the two agents.

"Come in. I assume there's something pressing I need to know about or else they wouldn't have flown you guys all the way the fuck out here."

He moved aside and let Rourke and Ben enter his home. Ben turned and put his hand out.

"Sir, I have to tell you what an honor it is to meet you. I'm the subject matter expert for the department and this is... "

Howl cut him off. "Save it, Irish. I ain't no judge and it ain't no honor, so quit kissin' my ass."

Ben frowned but Rourke couldn't help but smile a little. He'd rub it in Ben's face later. Never meet your heroes.

Howl led them through a long hallway decorated with various artifacts from the Golden Age. Rourke saw Ben practically drooling at The Mermaid's trident, the yellow and brown shield of The Protector, the entire costume of the Blue Projectile, and even the wood axe of Ireland's most famous superhero, Two-Ton Jack. Each piece was under glass and had a plaque telling its story. They were even numbered.

"I swear this place is more trouble than it's worth," Howl took a puff of his cigar. "If I were smart, I'd sell it and move back home to Jersey."

"Bayonne, right?" Ben offered. "Historians say you were born there."

"You know your stuff, but no. Hoboken. Grew up with Frank."

"Frank?" Ben puzzles.

"I think he means Sinatra," Rourke supplied.

"The very same. Little pipsqueak was always getting into trouble. Fell in with the wrong crowd." Howl chuckled, a gravelly, dry sound. "I shouldn't say wrong because they made him famous, yah know, but they were hoods. I never busted him though because he had a set of pipes on him."

Rourke smiled. "That he did."

"Frank knew how to party, that's for sure. I never got laid more than when he and I went to Vegas back when Vegas had class." He laughed again. They walked into the kitchen. "Where's yer buddy?"

Rourke turned around and saw that Ben was not behind him. "I think he got left behind back in that hallway museum you got there."

This time Howl guffawed. It wasn't a very pleasant sound, like rocks slamming together undercut by a slight wheeze. "Kid's star struck, I get it."

"Ben! We're waiting for you." Rourke called out.

"He has Two Ton Jack's axe, Rourke!"

Howl smiled. Surprisingly, it was a kind smile. He took a long drag on his cigar. "Shit, most people forgot about the Golden Age. It's sorta nice someone appreciates the good old days."

He led them to his kitchen table. The kitchen itself looked fairly clean, like it was barely used, it was a chef's kitchen but Rourke guessed no chef ever cooked there.

Howl gestured for them to sit.

"You fellas want a drink?" He took a deep breath, and before they had a chance to decline, bellowed, "CONSUELA!"

This led to a small coughing fit, and when he regained himself a bit he yelled again, "GODDAMN IT CONSUELA, GET DOWN HERE!"

Howl cleared his throat. "They send a different fucking housekeeper every few months and I can't keep track of 'em."

Rourke looked over a Ben, who looked uncomfortable. Rourke started, "Actually Mr. Howl... "

Suddenly, a young woman wearing jeans and a white blouse entered the kitchen; her black hair was tied back tightly.

"Yes, Mr. Howl?" Her accent was thick and Rourke couldn't place it.

"Darlin', mix up a batch of that tequila drink I like. The one with the orange juice in it and don't skimp on the hooch." Before she could answer, Howl slapped her on the butt. "That's a good girl."

Rourke winced. Ben shifted in his seat uncomfortably. The woman shook her head, rolled her eyes and did as he said.

"Do you typically drink before noon?" Ben asked.

"A black Irishman questioning someone about drinking? Now I've heard everything." Howl guffawed again. "Lemme guess, you're a vegetarian, too?"

"Mr. Howl..."

"Arnold," Howl interrupted. "Arnold Grant. That's my real name. The big secret identity."

"Arnold, if we could please get down to business. There's something pressing we need to discuss with you."

The woman came back with a pitcher and three short glasses.

"Thanks, doll." Howl gave her backside another pat. "Now beat it. Men are talking."

She left the kitchen hurriedly.

"Good girl but goddamn it if I don't understand a word coming out of her. She comes from one of them Mexican countries— Argentina or Brazil or some other third-world hell hole."

He poured three glasses of the tequila concoction and downed his in a single swallow.

"So, what's the scoop? What's the Golden Age Task Force want with little old me?"

He took a silver lighter from his pocket. His cigar had gone out. The lighter had a red wolf's head on it. Arnold lit the cigar and filled the kitchen with the smell of tobacco.

Rourke was no expert, but he was pretty sure it was Cuban. Director Hollis had a stash of old contraband Cubans in his desk and Rourke couldn't forget that sweet stink for the life of him.

"Arnold," Ben began, "the purpose of this visit is to inform you that we have it on good authority that your life may be in danger."

Arnold squinted and poured himself another drink, this time taking a small sip. "Wouldn't be the first time but I don't think anyone really cares enough to off me, so you'll have to excuse my skepticism."

"Parker McCoy is dead," Rourke said flatly. He took his glass and sipped his drink. The sharp taste of tequila filled his mouth. The orange juice didn't cut it at all.

For the first time, the man formerly known as The Crimson Howl looked concerned. He put his glass down slowly. He stubbed his cigar out on the table. It hissed.

"Parker McCoy is dead," he repeated. "How?"

"That's what we came here to talk to you about," Ben explained. "He was… eaten. Partially."

"What!?"

"Someone or something took a bite out of his abdomen. There were traces of black mold around the wound. We believe it was Deacon James."

Arnold took a long swallow of his drink. "Impossible. Deacon is dead. Got shot by feds in Vermont in '95. It was all over the news."

"We think it could have been either a copycat or that Deacon survived somehow. We're analyzing the mold we found around the bite. Should know in a few days." Rourke took another sip of his drink and decided he wouldn't have anymore. "Regardless of who killed Dr. McCoy there was a message on the wall that said, "Find Howl." Rourke produced his Nikon from his pocket and turned it on to show the picture of the message smeared in McCoy's blood and shit.

Howl's face turned cheese-white. He took the pitcher of the tequila mixture and drank deeply from it.

"He said he had it under control, the itch he called it." Arnold looked at the agents. "We believed him for so long. He was such a sweet kid."

Ben frowned "The itch?"

"It's what he'd call his compulsion to eat people." Howl elaborated. "We didn't know about it at first because he was able to hide it so well, but after working with him for a few years we began to notice him looking at people the way a hungry fella would look at a plate of steak and eggs." He took another long swallow from the pitcher. "Parker said he'd developed a serum to help his cravings but he must have stopped taking it in the Eighties because that's when the bodies started showing up with their guts ripped open and blood and shit smeared on the walls. Christ, I remember…"

CHAPTER FOUR

September 1984

He could sense something was off. They all could. None of this was right. And it was something beyond the blood splattered on the kitchen floor still being a little warm. Maybe it was because they were so close behind him.

The victim's belly was torn open wide and the insides had spilled. The intestines were torn in places. The stomach itself was completely missing. Probably eaten. Deacon James had developed a taste for guts, it seemed. It was relatively new.

Arnold Grant had thought he could smack some sense into Deacon. He considered it once or twice when Deacon's eyes would stare over the horizon to a place only he could see and the people they were collaring looked more like breakfast than burglars. Deacon was strong and strange and Arnold wasn't keen on laying his hands on the boy. Some things you just didn't mess around with.

It was Rudyard Sinclair who first noticed Deacon was starting to slip and he didn't have to put the Medallion of Delphi on to prove it.

"Something's wrong with him," Rudyard whispered. "I can't put my finger on it, and the Medallion won't show me but… something is off."

At the time, Arnold brushed it off. Deacon could be a little spooky on a good day. He was never one for conversation, never saying more than five words unless they were working. Even then, his voice was something of a sullen monotone, remaining perfectly flat at all times. He'd often stare out in the distance. The look on his face was one of a man having a conversation with himself. Rudyard said it was the black mold, that weird alien shit running through his bloodstream, speaking directly into Deacon's brain.

"It's obvious something's wrong with him but what do you want me to do about it?" Arnold had taken off his mask and helmet. "Christ, how are we going to cover this up?"

Deacon was still out there. More than likely going to hide out until the next time the craving hit. He…It? needed to be stopped, but that would have to wait until this was cleaned up. If the cops found the body like this, the trio of superheroes would lose control of things.

Troy Berlin cleared his throat. "I hate to be the one to say it but, why don't we just leave him here.?" He pointed to Deacon's latest victim. "It's not like the guy was an innocent victim. If you read the file we have on him, he was wanted for murder and statutory rape in three states and four counties. He was also, and I stress this, a Commie-loving son of a bitch."

Rudyard sneered. "You think that warrants a death sentence, don't you? God, you're a fucking psychotic."

Arnold got between them. "Fellas, let's dummy up a minute and…"

"What's a heathen sissy know about God, anyhow?" Troy snapped contemptuously.

Arnold was breathing heavily. Luck was still on his and Rudyard's side. No signs of Troy going haywire yet. They didn't need another bloodbath.

"I know enough. We've spoken many times." Rudyard half-smiled. "He called you an asshole on more than one occasion."

Troy's face went blank.

Arnold's stomach dropped. It was going to go bad now. It was just a matter of how bad.

To Arnold's complete surprise, Troy started laughing. It was a rich bellow. "You son of a bitch, that was a good one!" He slapped Rudyard on his back and the force of it sent Rudyard to his knees.

"Will you two idiots shut up and let me think?" Arnold yelled. "We got a serious problem here and you're bickering like a couple a' Mary's on a car ride." He stepped up to the body with no real enthusiasm.

The poor bastard's colon looked like a broken water balloon. Fecal matter and blood were mixed together as if a little kid had gotten into fingerpaints. Handprints and smears blotted the walls. Arnold saw a trail that led into the kitchen.

"Fellas, I think I got something here," he gestured and Troy and Rudyard followed.

"Man, that stinks!" Rudyard covered his nose. "I don't know how you can stand it, Howl. I got a regular sense of smell and I'm gaggin' on it."

"You'd know all about gagging on things, wouldn't you?" Troy snorted laughter.

Rudyard was about to respond when Arnold stopped dead in his tracks.

The walls in the kitchen were smeared with blood and shit just like the hallway leading into it, but there was something else, something that made The Crimson Howl's blood turn to ice water. Written in the victim's bodily fluids were the words:

SORRY
TASTE GOOD
HELP

This was going to have to be dealt with and dealt with quickly. If Deacon kept killing and eating suspected criminals, how long before he popped into a suburban home on Main Street U.S.A. and snacked on a housewife and her kid?

Deacon rarely spoke to them so it was hard to tell what was going on behind those faraway eyes and neutral smile. Howl assumed they would be safe because each of them knew how to defend themselves, but lately, as these incidents became more and more common, he wondered if they truly knew the extent of Deacon's abilities. It was one thing to work with a guy you couldn't

Written in the victim's bodily fluids...

get a real bead on. It was hard enough to deal with someone whose powers you didn't understand. The only thing worse than blind dates were blind team-ups.

"Shit," was all Howl said. The word hung in the air.

Rudyard and Troy were silent. Their jaws agape.

Finally: "This is new," Troy said. "It's obvious he wants to stop. This is proof. He wants us to help him."

Rudyard nodded. "It seems that way. It could also be a trap."

Troy rubbed his dimpled chin. "Why would it be a trap? You think he wants to eat us? We're his friends."

"Rudy might be on to something," Howl said. "Think about it, Troy."

"Yeah, use your brain for once," Rudyard grinned. "And stop calling me Rudy."

"I mean, you always said trusting a guy who never smiled was just as bad as trusting a guy who smiled too much," Howl recalled. "We don't even know how powerful Deacon really is?"

"When I put on the Medallion of Delphi, I saw the alien hiding inside of him. How it ran in his bloodstream. But there was something I couldn't see. Something the Medallion was unable to show me." Rudyard removed his turban, revealing a receding hairline.

Troy spoke. "You mean to tell me Deacon wants to lure us into some kind of trap to kill us and then eat us just like this guy and the other ones? Boys, you need to wise up. He's on our side, a good guy."

Rudyard let out a short laugh. It dripped with cynicism. "Troy old boy, that's what I adore about you. You still see things in black and white. I mean, you do realize we are nothing more than strongmen for the government. How many political dissidents have we had to beat the shit out of and throw in jail just because the higher-ups didn't like the cut of their jib? How many poor negroes did we have to …"

Before he had a chance to finish Howl barked, "Enough Rudyard!"

Troy's face went blank and only The Automatic Man was left.

Rudyard wouldn't have had a chance to dodge the punch even if he was prepared for it. Arnold himself barely saw the fist. The only thing he saw was a white and blue blur, and heard the sound of Rudyard's jaw being fractured in three places. Before Arnold had a chance to even try and break them up, Troy was raining blows on Rudyard's upper body with such speed Arnold was pretty sure Rudyard was going to be killed.

"Commie lovin' cock suckinmotherfuckin QUEER!" He was frothing at the mouth as he vomited expletives "niggerlovingsonofabitchin' FAGGOT!" More lightning-fast punches rained down upon Rudyard when suddenly Troy stopped. His face was a twisted fury of rage and confusion. Arnold looked on as the motionless body of Troy Berlin began to float above Rudyard's pummeled body.

Only it wasn't Rudyard's body at all. In fact, it had disappeared outright.

Arnold breathed a sigh of relief. "You can come out now Rudy"

Rudyard Sinclair, The Swami, walked slowly into the kitchen, the Medallion of Delphi draped around his neck gave off a light blue glow. "Is Troy all right?"

"He went haywire. You know you really shouldn't push his buttons like that."

Rudyard looked at the elevated body of the man who, just moments ago, was beating the shit out of a projection of himself. "His problem is, he can't see the big picture."

"You know that's not his fault," Arnold retorted. "And you know why it isn't."

Rudyard went over to Troy and patted his teammate on the shoulder. He gave him a pitying look. "The worst part is, I know this piece of shit would die for me if it came down to it. I know for a fact that when he's normal, I like him. A lot. But when he gets like this …"

Arnold finished for him. "When he gets like this you're a cocksuckin' queer and I'm a whoremongering porch-monkey fucker." The words sounded bad even to Arnold. "It's the same thing every time, Rudy. You have to let it go sometimes." He pointed his finger at Rudyard. "And stop pushing his buttons."

The Medallion of Delphi's light changed from blue to green and Troy was gently lowered to the ground. The light receded back to the Medallion and Troy snapped back to reality.

"Did I go haywire? Did I hurt anybody?" Troy stood up and brushed himself off. "What happened?"

Rudyard smiled and put his hand on Troy's shoulder. "You got mad, but no one got hurt."

Arnold nodded. "Yeah. Look we gotta figure out what the hell we're going to do with the body and how we're going to explain this to the Feds."

Troy smiled. "Leave that to me."

CHAPTER FIVE

The kitchen was filled with a dense cloud of cigar smoke. Arnold Grant had gone through five cigars already. He had also moved on from the Tequila concoction his housekeeper made to just drinking it straight. If he was even the slightest bit drunk, he didn't show it.

"That was back in Eighty-Four, I think. We eventually caught up to Deacon in a tenement house in Philadelphia." He took a swig from the bottle of Patron. "It was Rudyard who caught him in the act. Thing about Rudy was, he had seen all kinds of spooky shit in his day. That Medallion of his was the genuine article so he was used to seeing dead people, demons, and all kinds of shit when he put it on. But this? Seeing Deacon for what he truly was scared the ever-loving fuck outta Rudyard Sinclair. I think he aged ten years that night and guys like us, well, look at me, we don't hardly age."

He passed his bottle to Rourke, who declined. Ben shrugged and took a sip. He had been scribbling furiously since Howl started telling them his story. Rourke half-expected the papers to be little hearts with Ben's and Arnold's names in them. He was proud of Ben though, he was doing his level best not to stare starry-eyed and slack-jawed.

Howl noticed Ben taking frantic notes and snorted. "Kid, what the hell are you doin'?"

"This is important," Ben stated. "It's for my research."

"Well, I got a million stories. Thing is, I don't have any clue why Deacon James is gunning for me."

"That is what we're trying to find out, too," Rourke fanned away the cigar smoke. "Do you keep in touch with your old partners, Troy and, uhm, Rudyard?"

Howl shrugged. "Not really. I mean, I get a Christmas card from Vera every year. Vera is Troy's wife. She sends me a card and I don't write back."

"And Rudyard Sinclair?" Ben asked.

"Fucked if I know where Rudy is. Last I heard, and this was some years ago, he was telling fortunes on the boardwalk in Jersey."

"For all you know they could be dead, just like Parker McCoy," Rourke offered.

Howl nodded. "Could be. I doubt it, though."

"What makes you say that?" Rourke asked.

Howl took a long drag on what was now his sixth cigar. He exhaled slowly, tapping his fingers on the counter. "Because those two sumbitches ain't particularly easy to kill. That goes for me too. If Deacon really is trying to find me, then he's probably in trouble."

Rourke coughed a little. "Or, he really wants to kill you like he did McCoy."

"Maybe, little man. But tell me somethin', son. What's his end game? Why after all these years would he go about killing the only people who made him feel normal? Why would he want to murder Parker McCoy in the first place? Why him and not a random stranger?"

Ben looked up from his notes. "Maybe it's not Deacon James. Maybe it's the alien inside of him. That weird mold thing."

"You have to admit it's a real possibility," Rourke concurred.

They fell silent. It was cut by the sound of a ringing landline phone. It was answered by the housekeeper. Howl looked over his shoulder and raised his eyebrow.

"That's funny. Ain't nobody knows my home number."

"You never gave it out to anyone?" Rourke queried.

"Naw. I got it as part of some bundle package from those cable crooks. Told em' to keep the number private, too."

Consuela entered the kitchen holding a cordless phone. Her face was all wrinkles and confusion.

"Well?" Howl growled. "Who the hell is it?"

"Mr. Howl, they say it's for you."

Arnold got up and snatched it away from her and went out into the hallway.

"I think I'm gonna die of lung cancer if we stay here any longer," Rourke coughed.

"But isn't it great? Isn't he great?" Ben was all smiles. "That story, I bet you every word of it was true. I can't wait to cross-reference it with my files back in Washington."

Arnold came back into the kitchen and put the phone down on the table. He sighed deeply grabbed the bottle of Patron and took a healthy swig.

"Everything all right?" Ben inquired.

Silence for a moment. "That was Troy Berlin. Haven't spoken to him in damn near twenty years. He just found out about Parker McCoy."

"How did he get your number?" Rourke asked. "And more importantly, how the hell did he find out about McCoy?"

"He still has contacts in the government. They don't forget about old heroes... at least not when they're like us." He took another long swallow, finishing the bottle. "He wanted to know if I knew anything about it. He sounded a little worried."

"Why would he be worried? What was his relationship to McCoy?" Ben twirled the pen in his hand.

Arnold stood and went over to the far cabinet to the right of the table and took out a new bottle of tequila. "Troy Berlin was one of Parker McCoy's first test subjects."

"That makes sense." Rourke looked over and saw Ben start taking notes again. "For the record, we are allowed to write this down as part of an ongoing investigation."

Arnold chuckled. "Sure. Just make sure I get twenty percent of the gross when the fucking book comes out." He wrenched open the new bottle and took a swig "Troy was an enlisted man in the army in thirty-nine. Good old FDR must have been looking eastward because that strudel fuckin' kraut in Germany was causing all kinds of trouble. Annexing this and invading that.

He knew he'd have to do something about it and met with McCoy in secret about a project he was working on. Basically, he'd figured out a way to alter genetics to make someone a better human being."

Ben looked up from his notepad. "They knew about advanced genetic manipulation back in Thirty-Nine?"

Rourke raised an eyebrow. "Yeah, didn't they crack the human genome in the Nineties or something?"

Arnold dismissed them with a wave. "McCoy knew all about that shit before the invention of color television. Guy was a fuckin' genius. Made that cripple with the voice box look like a caveman." He paused for a drink. "Anyway, the story goes, Troy signed up for this project. The two of them became friends and when I gained notoriety for cleaning up Bayonne, it was only a matter of time before we joined forces."

"So, Troy knew McCoy before you did?" Rourke surmised.

"Uh-huh. From what I understand they did nearly a year's worth of experiments on him and a few other guys. Troy, it turned out, was a great test subject. Responded to all the tests and shit while the other guys either dropped out of the program or..." He trailed off.

Ben looked up. "Or?"

"Or had strange things happen to them. Some of them became deformed; others just went crazy because the scientists did stuff to the part of their genes that affected their heads. A few killed themselves. All but Troy. Except for that one part."

Rourke nodded. "I was going to ask you about that. You said he goes 'haywire'. Was that part of McCoy's genetic manipulation?"

"Naw. That was a different program. It was some kind of brainwashing program the OSS conjured up. They performed brain surgery on him. Fuckin' lunatics. It was so in case he got captured he wouldn't be able to divulge information or some shit. All it did was make him go blank and he'd go berserk. Tearing into anyone and anything. It was terrible to see him like that."

"His wife must be terrified of him," Ben deduced.

"You'd think so, but he never laid a hand on her," Arnold continued. "Or his kids. Don't know how he did it, but with them, he's perfectly normal. Anyone else, you take your fuckin' chances."

There was silence except for the sound of pen on paper.

Rourke leaned back in his chair, watching Ben write. He noticed Grant watching Ben too, the old vigilante smirking at something. Rourke's expression soured. Ben believed he never read any of the files. He read them, even the ones so redacted all that was left was a name and a mailing address. What was the point of having a pair of stooges sitting around on the taxpayer dime unable to get anything done? Ben could usually figure out everything about a case from the barest scraps, but Rourke was less amused. If this old hack couldn't help them, maybe Troy could.

"Arnold, you think Troy would be up for a visit?" Rourke proposed. "I think it would be a good idea to question him, as well. You know, to maybe find out a possible motive."

Howl shot a not particularly kind look at Rourke. "Son, why the hell do you wanna open up that can a' worms?"

"Because I think maybe Troy might know something. A reason for McCoy's murder. If he's still got resources that can tell him about a hush-hush government investigation, maybe he's heard something we haven't. I don't know, but I think it's worth dropping in on him." Rourke looked at Ben for support.

Ben merely shrugged.

Howl squinted at him "You think Troy knows anything?"

"It's possible," Rourke answered. "Maybe he and Deacon are in on it together. I mean, what did the two of you really talk about for the few minutes you were on the phone with him? Hell, maybe all three of you are in on it."

Ben cleared his throat, "Rourke doesn't mean to . . ."

Arnold stiffened, "No, Irish, I think he means to. I think he absolutely means to." In a flash Grant was reaching across, grabbing Rourke by his shirt and tie. "You listen to me, you little runt of a shit. Parker McCoy was a lot of things. He could be a stone-cold son of a bitch, but he was my friend and he was Troy's, too. If you think for one second he'd. . ."

There was an audible click as Ben pulled the hammer back on his gun.

"Let him go." Ben's voice shook slightly. "I don't want to have to shoot you."

"Something tells me he isn't bulletproof, Ben."

Howl eased off and let Rourke go. Then he pounded his fist on the table. "Goddamn, if I wasn't buzzed, I woulda' knocked you both out before you had a chance to yell fer ya' momma." Then he laughed. "Must be getting old."

"Thought you said that didn't really happen to your type." Rourke stood up and straightened his tie and shirt. "I think we're just about done here."

"Now wait a second fellas," Howl held up his hand. "Look, I didn't want to snap at ya' that way but you gave me no choice."

"Listen, as far as I'm concerned, we did our jobs. We found you and warned you. We're not under any other obligation to help you." Rourke's face was hot. "Come on, Ben. We're going to have to visit Troy Berlin. See if he knows anything about any of this."

Ben rose slowly and Arnold stood up, too. "Now wait a second, kid. You don't even know where Troy lives."

Rourke whipped out his smartphone, "I got Google. I can figure it out."

"Rourke, wait a second," Ben said.

"What?"

Ben glanced over at Arnold. "I think seeing Troy is a good idea but how will he react seeing two Federal Agents at his doorstep? If what Arnold said was true just the mere sight of us could be enough to make him go crazy. I don't know about you, but I'm not faster than the Human Bullet."

"Irish makes a lot of sense," Arnold agreed. "I haven't seen the guy in twenty years, but I knew him well in the old days. If you're gonna go to his house without knowing the rules you're basically signing your death warrant."

Rourke looked at Arnold. "Rules?"

Arnold smiled. "Sure. Let me pack. We got a long drive to New Mexico."

Ben looked confused. "Drive?"

"If you think I'm getting on a plane next to some camel humpin' A-Rab you got another thing comin'. I ain't bulletproof, your partner here was right about that, and I ain't bombproof neither."

Rourke rolled his eyes. "Great. We get to play nanny to the Exceptional version of Archie Bunker. Hurry up and pack. Don't forget your adult diaper, what with you getting old and all."

Arnold walked over to Rourke and leaned in close. "Boy, when this is over, you and me are gonna tussle. You ain't gonna like how it ends."

CHAPTER SIX

The sun rose to greet the denizens of the Red Oak Trailer Park just like any other day including Roger Rapowski. The blackout curtains blocked out the sun in his metal shitbox. His home was a labyrinth of clutter: stacks of old newspapers blocked the narrow hallways. Boxes of junk—though it wasn't junk to Roger because it all had value to him—were stacked too high and too deep and took up most, if not all of the living room.

As he got older Roger found it very difficult to get rid of all the treasures he found on his daily walk to work. Truth be told, he found it difficult to get out of bed anymore. Often, he'd wake up in the middle of the night, with a dire urge to take the biggest piss of his life gripping his bladder only, to squeeze out a drop or two. Roger's routine would start each morning with hacking up black and brown wads of phlegm. He'd spit them into the old coffee can beside his weary and soiled mattress.

He awoke to the sound of Vasilli, making a retching sound. The cat had been getting worse and it might be time to finally put him down.

He got up slowly. His normal coughing fit wasn't as bad this morning but his back ached and he had slept wrong so his neck was all out of whack. He took a look at himself in the dirty, greasy, smoke-stained mirror.

His skin was a sickly yellow, matching his teeth, and dark purple bags drooped like slugs under his eyes. What little hair he had left was past his shoulders, held together by an old rubber band.

Vasilli made another retching noise. Roger looked down and saw the old Maine Coon looking up at him. The cat was losing its gray and black fur in places. Often Roger would pet the poor wretch and clumps of fur would come off, leaving bare skin. It had lost more than a few teeth and Roger noticed he didn't purr anymore. Probably because Vasilli's vocal cords had deteriorated after twenty years around the same time his organs stopped working.

He looked over at his cracked alarm clock. He had work in an hour and it was a pretty far walk from the trailer park. He had to get moving.

He had slept in his clothes so he was halfway ready but a tiny rumble in his increasingly decreasing belly told him he should eat. He carefully put down Vasilli, who darted behind a stack of old issues of Weekly World News and Human Bullet comics, tiptoed around the four dirty hampers filled with mold that resembled clothes, and cautiously made his way into his equally filthy kitchen and grabbed a can of chili from the counter and a semi-clean spoon from the stopped-up sink.

Roger turned and looked at his kitchen table, the only thing in his hovel of a trailer that was clean. On it lie scientific instruments, a brand-new microscope, beakers, and a Bunsen burner. On each chair sat small drums of industrial chemicals. He smiled absently through chapped lips and didn't know why.

He finished his can of chili and threw it in the overflowing garbage can under the sink put on his jacket and walked out the door and into the fresh air. It made him cough.

Usually, Roger enjoyed his walks to work, but lately, some of the trailer park kids would follow him. Snickering and holding their noses as they passed him on their scooters or bikes. They called him Old Codger Roger and once or twice one of the little shits threw garbage at him. They would wait to see if Roger would pick it up and put it in his pocket and would mock him when he did.

Today, a few of the little wastes of semen decided to up their game. Two boys, no more than thirteen years waited for him by the stop sign by the Red Oak entrance.

"Hey Codger!" the first boy called. "You fuckin' stink!" He produced something from his pocket. Roger didn't see it coming until it was too late.

The little fuck sprayed him with deodorant. The second boy also produced something from his pockets and let loose full force. One whizzed past and clanged against Roger's trailer.

Rocks! Fucking rocks now!

The kid couldn't throw for shit and none of the rocks hit Roger but damn it if that deodorant didn't reek. Before Roger could react, the kids were up, up, and away on their bikes, howling with malicious laughter.

If these were the old days those two snot-nosed pukes would be dealt with in a most un-pleasant manner. He walked, keeping his head down. Sometimes a treasure or two would be left by the curb after trash day and he would quickly scoop it up and shove it in his pocket. Sometimes, and these were the best, he'd find a dead bird on the side of the road. He'd have to leave it someplace where nothing would get at it since he couldn't carry it around for an eight-hour shift. On the way home, he'd go back to where he'd hid it and toss it in his freezer with the rest of them.

No such luck today.

Before he knew it, he had turned the corner which led to the Hazlet Costco shopping center on state route 35.

Roger rushed across the wide road when the light turned. Even walking that quickly left him winded on the other side. At least now he was at the entrance of the massive parking lot which housed not just his Costco, but a fancy movie theater and some disgusting Italian restaurant.

He patted his jacket pocket, searching for his Pall Malls but couldn't find them. He looked over his shoulder and saw that they had fallen out as he crossed the highway. Before he had a chance to retrieve them a green Prius ran them over, crushing their tobacco guts onto the road.

A rash of irritation spread in Roger. It was one of those days now, wasn't it? He was no longer who he once was. He was Roger Rapowski, a humble casket salesman at the Hazlet, New Jersey Costco.

He sighed and walked the lonely walk into the wholesale store employee entrance. Usually, people were bustling around and avoided him outright. That was okay with Roger. He wasn't much of a people person anyway. He went over to the time clock and punched in. He went over to the men's room to take a pre-shift piss but found the entrance blocked by his immediate supervisor.

Frank was a portly little man, with an easy smile and thinning hair that reminded most folks of Friar Tuck from the old Robin Hood movies. He wore a checkered shirt and black jeans.

"Roger. I've got some bad news," He said. He handed Roger a manila envelope with his name on it. "This store is no longer selling caskets or funeral-related items, so …"

"I'm fired." The words hung in the air for a moment.

"I'm afraid so," Frank pointed to the envelope, "Everything you need to know about filing for unemployment is in there."

Roger looked at the envelope and shrugged slightly. He turned and walked out of the employee area and back outside and made his way back to the Red Oak Trailer Park.

CHAPTER SEVEN

He arrived home to the sound of his landline telephone ringing a broken warbling tone. He didn't own a cell phone because the reception interfered with the work on the table. What was he working on again? He remembered the ringing and remembered that his number was unlisted. He quickly unlocked the door, stumbled through a stack of magazines, and answered it.

"'llo?" he said, his voice barely a whisper.

"Roger Rapowski?" The voice on the other end was deep but fake. It was one of those anonymous TV show caller voices, all static and garble.

"Who's this?"

"A friend. I have need of your talents," the deep, fake voice said. "There is a body at the Bayshore Community Hospital not too far from your house. Tonight, at three-thirty I need you to retrieve it."

Roger's pulse quickened.

"What body?"

"You'll know it when you see it," the voice said. "Are you up to the task? You will be compensated handsomely for your time."

He didn't want to seem too eager. He settled on a neutral "Sure."

"Good," the voice concluded. "The Exceptionals are returning. An alarm is ringing."

The line went dead. Roger hung up. He smiled wide and looked down at the envelope in his hand. He tossed it on the counter with all the other mail, magazines, and junk that had piled up over the years. He wouldn't need it.

No. The first thing he would need is a shower. A good, long, hot shower. The comeback special was tonight and he wanted to be clean. He looked at his fingernails, nicotine-stained and thick and in dire need of a trim. He ran from the kitchen into his bedroom, knocking over piles of old newspapers and boxes of his treasures. Treasures? Trash. Today was his birthday and Christmas and his first blowjob all at the same time. Tonight, Roger, Roger the Codger would die and all that would be left was who he really, honestly and truly was.

For tonight, by the light of the full moon, The Mortician would make his triumphant comeback.

•••

Roger showered and dried, a spring in his step as he went from the bathroom to his bedroom. He threw his tiny closet door open. It was empty except for a single garment bag, a shoe box, and a hat box. He carefully took the garment bag out of and put it on the bed and slowly opened it, revealing its contents.

It was a black mourning suit; the kind undertakers wore back in the old days, when people still took pride in their work. A crisp, white shirt with black buttons hung on a separate hanger, the sleeves ended with a pair of cufflinks that looked like red teardrops. Folded neatly and clipped to the hanger were clean black dress socks and black boxers. He put the shirt on and fumbled with the buttons, cursing under his breath. He gingerly tied the tie, his fingers finally gaining flexibility. He slid into his boxers and his pants. They hung from him like a widow's dress in all the places he had lost weight. Luckily, he had a belt lying around somewhere.

Roger breathed heavily, reached into the bag, and pulled out his mourning suit coat. He buttoned all but the bottom button. Last, but never least to Roger, no, to The Mortician, was the hat-box. He placed his hands on the box with reverence and gently put it on his dresser (not before swiping all the junk off.) He slowly opened the hatbox and pulled out the black top hat. His eyes welled with tears. He never thought he'd ever wear it again. He had forgotten it, somehow. He put the hat on. It smelled first like mothballs, then, like the old days.

He was crying hard now. Memories came in droves; dreams of fighting the heroes, of raising his army of undead to strike terror into the hearts of the weak and innocent; his dearest animals, the glee of torturing someone with their dead loved ones.

He sniffed as more tears fell. The last piece of his costume, of himself was a red tiepin. It was a ruby carved into the likeness of a laughing skull.

He turned and looked in the dirty mirror. He gasped. For a moment, he was much younger. Like himself when things were good and there were enemies to fight and horror to bring into the world. He smiled; his chapped lips cracked and oozed dark blood. He licked them smooth and red. The tears stopped. There was only one thing missing.

"Vasilli!" He shouted; his voice as clear as a bell and full of triumphant menace. "TO ME, MY PET!"

The cat made a retching sound and obeyed his master. He jumped from the bed to the dresser and up on Roger's right shoulder.

Very nimble for a dead cat.

The Mortician let out a laugh, a bellow full of mischief and menace.

He went back to the hatbox and pulled out two other pieces of equipment. A black cigarette holder about six inches long and an old perfume bottle, one of those old-fashioned jobs with the rubber squeezer at the one end. He'd no doubt have to mix up a special batch of immobilizer before his job tonight. He sauntered into the makeshift lab his kitchen table had become and got to work.

Despite his giddiness, The Mortician's hands were steady as he mixed the chemicals which would render his victims helpless and hypnotized, with no memory of seeing him or his long-dead feline companion. A squirt directly in the face would do the trick. Getting into the hospital unnoticed wouldn't be much trouble. He carefully poured the batch of immobilizer into the perfume bottle and pumped the rubber squeezer. It came out in a mist.

Perfect. Now to find an unwitting fool to get him to where he needed to go.

•••

The ride to Bayshore hospital only took ten minutes. The Mortician's pulse sped up as he waited for the paramedics to open the doors. Vasilli stood atop his shoulder.

Killing the two boys who had ambushed him earlier was easy. He revived a dead owl from his freezer using another cocktail of chemicals and sicked it on the little bastards. Tearing lumps of flesh from their heads and faces until arteries were cut and blood spurted in hot jets. It was The Mortician who called for the ambulance and when the meat wagon had arrived, he descended on the paramedics, who were now under his chemical control.

"Take these bodies and throw them in that dumpster there."

Without speaking the two paramedics did as they were told. The bodies of the two boys were thrown into the dumpster near the ambulance area. They returned to the ambulance to find The Mortician on the stretcher inside the unzipped body bag.

"Good," The Mortician said. "Zip this bag up. You will wheel me into the morgue."

Again, the paramedics did as they were told. One of them zipped up the bag and The Mortician—Vassili between his legs—was wheeled down to the morgue where a body was waiting for him. The paramedics spoke with the security guard and were buzzed in. When the door closed, the body bag was opened and The Mortician rose from it like the ghoul he used to be.

"Excellent," he hissed. Vassili joined his master on his shoulder. "Now to find the body. Open these cold chambers and let's see what we have here."

Methodically, his hypnotized slaves opened the row of six corpse doors and pulled out the bodies. The Mortician drummed his fingers together and smiled. It was too bad there weren't any Exceptionals around anymore. He would have loved to rumble with The Swami or the Blue Projectile or even . . .

"Parker McCoy!?"

Rigor mortis had subsided hours ago and his face no longer held a look of horror but one of lifeless indifference. A milky white sheen covered his eyes and the faint smell of blood and shit perfumed the air.

Who the hell took a bite out of his abdomen?

He snapped his fingers and one of the paramedics walked over to him.

"Get the stretcher and place this body in the body bag. We're going home."

The paramedic obliged and lifted the semi-frozen body of Parker McCoy. "Gently with him." The Mortician cautioned. "He need not spill what is left of his guts."

Once McCoy was safely tucked away, The Mortician zipped the bag up.

Now to get out unnoticed.

The paramedics stood motionless save for their breathing. Their faces were complete blanks.

He gestured to the paramedics and they wheeled the body out of the morgue. The Mortician took out his perfume bottle. The security guard would have to be dealt with. Vasilli retched again.

The door to the morgue opened slowly. Vasilli ran in front of The Mortician over to the desk where the security guard sat and gave a hiss.

Before the guard had a chance to give a startled yelp he was sprayed in the face with a mist of immobilizer. The guard's face turned blank and the trio went past unnoticed.

•••

With a strength he had forgotten he had, he carried the body of Parker McCoy into his filthy trailer. He sent the ambulance on its way on the wrong side of the highway where it was smashed into by a garbage truck. Killing both paramedics and the truck driver, as well.

It didn't occur to him that someone had unlocked his front door. He nearly dropped the body bag when he saw a figure standing amongst his filth.

"Don't turn on the light," the voice said. It sounded just like the voice on the phone. "Hand over the body."

The Mortician squinted. "Who are you?"

"That…is unimportant at the moment. The body, please," the voice said.

"I was told I would be rewarded for my work."

The figure pointed over to the spotless kitchen table. A metal briefcase sat next to his lab equipment. "One million dollars in cash. I think you'll find it an adequate start to the work we are going to do together."

At first, the words didn't register. Couldn't be right.

"Did you say…"

Hand over the body

"Yes," the voice confirmed. "Now, there is an address on the inside of that case. In seven days, you will join me there. Understood?"

The Mortician nodded.

"Good." The figure stepped out of the darkness to the relative light of the porch.

The Mortician's eyes went wide. "You!?"

The figure grinned. He put his finger to his lips. "Shhh." He winked and, surprisingly, lifted the body of Parker McCoy with little effort and was gone.

The Mortician removed his hat and bolted to the kitchen table. He hastily opened the briefcase and smiled wide. On top of the stacks of hundred-dollar bills lay a pack of Pall Malls.

The son of a bitch was good.

He took out his cigarette holder and put one of the smokes in. He lit it with a match. Vasilli nuzzled his master's neck. A chunk of his fur fell to the floor.

He glanced at the top of the briefcase. Taped to it was the address he would have to meet his friend to begin whatever work they had to do.

The Mortician glanced around his trailer. Suddenly it looked…different. What was all this garbage doing here? Boxes of magazines? Why the hell would he want to keep these things? His house was fucking filthy. He squinted, "This will not do, Vasilli. Let us depart this loathsome hovel for…gloomier pastures."

The Mortician threw his head back and laughed.

CHAPTER EIGHT

It took three hours just to get out of L.A. Sitting and stewing in the California heat wasn't something Rourke and Ben were used to.

Their companion, the once and former Crimson Howl, had dozed off an hour into their journey. Rourke had a mental list of Grant's charming quirks: insufferable drunk, reeked of stale cigars, unapologetic racist —although the old bastard might just hate everyone— and now he could add "snores like a rusty buzz-saw."

"I still can't believe we aren't on a fucking plane right now," Rourke's frustration oozed through clenched teeth. "We'd be there already."

They had abandoned their rental car back at Arnold's because the old crime fighter refused to ride in a "Jap" car and insisted they take his personal ride instead. A vintage 1967 red and black Dodge Charger.

"I'm sorry, but this was the only way we'd get him to come along," Ben had opted to drive because he had the least to drink back at Arnold's house.

"We didn't need him to come," Rourke argued. "He invited himself on our investigation for Christ's sake." He folded his arms.

Arnold snored.

"Jesus, that sound goes right through me." Rourke shivered.

It wasn't that Rourke didn't have a point. They probably didn't need to have Arnold with them, but according to the case files, the Human Bullet or the Automatic Man or Whatever The Fuck He Called Himself could snap because you looked at him the wrong way. For as excited as Ben was to meet one of the most famous Exceptional of all time, Rourke didn't want to say the wrong thing and have The Automatic Man go "haywire" on him.

"He said there were rules we had to follow when we meet Troy Berlin," Ben reminded Rourke. "It may be the difference between us getting what we need or ending up in full body casts."

Rourke snorted. "Rules? It's all bullshit, Ben. These clowns are nothing more than a bunch of overgrown boys playing dress-up. Besides, I'm sure by now Berlin's reflexes have slowed down enough that if we had to take him down, we could. Guy is pushing what, Ninety? He may be as fast as a bullet, but I didn't read anything in his file about him being bulletproof."

Ben shook his head, "I'd prefer not to find out."

"How long is it going to take to get there again?" Rourke asked a second time.

Ben glanced down at the GPS on his phone. "A while."

After about another twenty-five minutes or so of stop-and-go, the traffic started moving and they were on their way.

The Dodge rumbled along, wanting to go much faster than thirty-five miles per hour but unable to because of all the slowly moving unclogging traffic.

They were finally picking up speed when Arnold woke up.

A few minutes later they were doing sixty-five heading towards I-40. Rourke looked out the window. Some fair-weather clouds blotted out the California sun intermittently. He noticed a few drivers would point at them as they passed. A few tried to stupidly take pictures with their phone. They knew it was The Crimson Howl and wanted a good look. Arnold grinned and rolled down the window and waved at a car full of girls.

"This sort of thing common when you go out in this car?" Rourke asked.

"All the fuckin' time, pipsqueak!" Arnold's grin grew larger resembling a jack o' lantern. He waved at another group of people. This time some Asian tourists. His smile quickly faded. "Fuckin' Japs," he mumbled quickly putting his hand back in the car.

"How do you know they're Japanese?" Rourke quizzed.

Ben looked over his shoulder and gave him a look.

Rourke smiled mischievously.

Arnold rolled up his window and looked over his shoulder. "I know a Jap when I see one."

Rourke laughed. "That's funny, they looked Korean to me."

"Oh, so you can tell one yellow monkey from another, huh?"

"Much in the same way you can tell that a person of Asian descent must be Japanese. I guess it's my exceptional ability. You know, you remind me of Archie Bunker. Except I don't think Archie would have been caught dead wearing a wolf mask and a cape. I think he'd consider that …Faggy."

Arnold's face turned a light shade of red, "Now listen here yah fuckin' liberal P.C. dipshit…"

"For a second I thought you were going to call me meathead," Rourke could sense Ben getting uncomfortable. "C'mon, man. I was only fuckin' with you. Geez, can't a guy have a little fun on this accidental road trip you're insisting we go on?"

"Yeah." Ben chimed in quickly. "He was only messing with you, best to pay him no mind. I know I don't. Jackass that he is."

There was a moment of silence. Arnold exhaled sharply through his nose. "Alright, I'll let it go this time, but pipsqueak, remember what I said. When this is all over, you and me are gonna go at it."

The Dodge picked up speed to 85. It was going to be a long way to New Mexico. He wondered what would happen when they reached Troy Berlin, the Human Bullet sometimes called The Automatic Man. How was he going to fit into all of this?

And just where was Deacon James hiding out and what were they going to do when they finally caught him?

CHAPTER NINE

They pulled into a truckstop a few hours later at Arnold's insistence. Though Ben was eager to keep driving. He could tell Rourke was getting more and more impatient with each passing mile. Nor could Ben ignore the rumbling in his stomach or the fullness of his bladder. Once both urges were satisfied, they got back into the car and made their way down I-40 toward New Mexico.

"What a fuckin' dump," Arnold commented, breaking a five-minute silence. "If it were the old days, we woulda' had the best fuckin' table in that joint."

"I don't think there was a best table anywhere in that shit-hole." Rourke had taken Ben's place in the driver's seat. "Steak and eggs were good, though."

Arnold grunted in agreement. "Back in the olden days, us Exceptionals would haunt the diners until the sun came up. Usually, we'd all start around sundown— those of us on Uncle Sam's dime— that is. We'd go on patrol until four or five in the morning, bustin' heads and collarin' crooks. A lot of us would congregate around five thirty or so for breakfast. Shit, you'd have ten or twenty guys sitting around swapping stories of the night's adventures. Who fought which supervillain, how many teeth got knocked out of some would-be rapist. We'd raise hell in those diners till eight or nine in the morning and take home a gal or two and do it all over again the next day. Those were some good days, fellas. Real good days."

From the back seat Ben nodded. The thought of seeing a bunch of costumed heroes sitting around chewing the fat while eating buttered toast and fried eggs made him smile. He took out a small notebook from his coat pocket. "Would you mind if I wrote that down? I'd like it for my files."

Arnold smiled, "Of course ya can, Irish." He looked at Rourke, "You can learn a lot from this guy. He respects his elders."

Rourke kept his eyes on the road

"I like yah, Irish." Arnold continued. "If I didn't already have a ghostwriter, I'd ask you to do it. Shit, maybe I'll fire the Jew sonofabitch and hire you for when we've figured out this whole thing with Deacon. I'm sure my adoring fans would love to hear about it."

Ben grimaced. "I'm afraid that because of the nature of this mission it'll remain classified for a few decades regardless of the outcome."

"Heh, there's always ways around that shit," Arnold suggested.

"Something's been bugging me, Arnold," Rourke interjected.

Arnold rolled his eyes. "Why ain't I surprised?"

"No, really. It's bothered me since I joined the Task Force. Why did all the supervillains just up and stop getting up to trouble? It seemed like when Congress repealed the Exceptional People's Act they'd be free to run amok but they didn't."

Arnold thought a moment. "You know, I never really gave it much thought. I like to figure it was because, without guys like us, it wasn't fun anymore."

"But these guys were into some serious stuff like espionage and trying to take over the world. Things like that, right?" Ben wondered never looking up from his notebook.

Arnold nodded. "A lot of the diner guys were just small-time hoods who saw what we were doing and wanted in on the action. The big-time guys were like me and Troy and Rudyard and Deacon. Working for rival government agencies.

"That ain't to say we didn't have a tough time with the small-fry crooks. There was a few of 'em that we rumbled with on a regular basis. There was a guy called himself the Brown Bomber. Negro. Had a thing for high explosives and blowing up white lunch counters and the like. The guys in Harlem, they didn't consider him a villain, yah know. He was a fuckin' hero to those guys but it was a different time back then and we had to take him out."

"You killed him?" Ben blurted out.

"Naw! We busted his head up something awful. Troy whooped him so badly he never walked right again. Got sent upstate to some looney bin. Nothing like that little asshole Sergeant Seppuku. He was a Jap kid who was pissed we dropped the A-bomb on his shithole country. He could make people kill themselves. Nasty bastard liked collecting the heads of white women." Arnold shook his head. "Him we had to put down."

"Jesus," Ben said, "did you have to…put down a lot of those guys?"

Arnold grunted a laugh. "Only the guys who deserved it. See, some guys put on the costume for different reasons. They figure it gives them an identity, and makes them a someone in a sea of nobodies. Mostly the bad guys were just guys who were down on their luck or mad at the world because their politics didn't fit into the grand scheme of things here in America. Problem was, you'd bust the guy's head and throw him and jail for a while and they'd come back to haunt you a few months or a few years later. I can't tell yah how many times I had to throw Mister Titanium in the clink. Every six months or so I'd have to beat the shit out of him and throw him in jail."

There was a pause.

"Of course, some of these guys…well, one of 'em learned his lesson. There was a kid in the fifties who called himself Comrade Gulag. He was a small-timer from Brooklyn. He'd blow up cars and attack people while spouting Commie nonsense. Dressed up like the goddamned Soviet flag and even had a picture of that cocksucker Lenin over his heart. We caught wind of it and found out where he was and busted his head and threw him in jail."

"Then what happened?" Ben wanted to know.

"About three months after that I got a letter. Don't ask me how the kid got my address but I got it anyway. He was in Sing-Sing doing a year for assault. He told me that he was grateful, glad even, that me and Troy and Rudyard came to Brooklyn and beat the stuffing out of him. He said his mother was so ashamed of him that she couldn't look at him during his sentencing and he'd had enough of spreading that evil commie shit. When he got out, he said, he was going to go straight and stay straight."

"And I assume he did?" Ben kept jotting down notes.

"I tell yah, the kid was as good as his word." Arnold grinned proudly. "He'd write me every so often saying how good he was doin' and thankin' me up and down. When he got out, he got a job working on the docks. It was easier back then for a guy with a record to get a job. He worked his way up to foreman and then head of the Dock Workers Union. Made a good living and carved out a nice piece of the American Dream. He got married to a nice girl. Lydia was her name. She'd send me these homemade rum balls every Christmas. Boy, they were delicious. Every year I'd get a tin and every year there'd be a card attached. All it said was 'thank you'. He had six kids and a slew of grandkids."

"What happened to him?" Ben looked up.

Arnold waved his hand. "Ah, he died peacefully in ninety-two surrounded by his wife and family. His name was Alexi Anatoly. I got a letter in ninety-five from his oldest daughter, this was when Lydia died. She said her dad always told his kids the story about when the Crimson Howl broke his head and put him in jail. She said it helped keep her and her brothers and sisters out of trouble and thanked me one last time for what I'd done." Arnold paused and smirked. "So it wasn't all bad."

"What else happened back then? I mean, you've got to be full of stories." Ben knew he had the old hero on a roll.

"Well, I'm sure you read my tell-all."

"Three times."

Arnold laughed. "Three times!? Shit kid, yah shoulda' brought it with you. I woulda' signed it. Hell. I like yah, Irish."

Ben was practically beaming.

"I tell yah, it was great back then," Arnold's voice was full of pride. "Aside from a few politicians in Washington, we didn't have to answer to nobody. The mob feared us, women loved us and every Tom, Dick, and Harry tried to copy us. We were the real deal, though. We were the fuckin' genuine article. When fake tough guys like The Soviet Crusher and the Dragon came around lookin' for trouble, they didn't call out the National Guard. They called us. The fuckin' Exceptionals. We handled the jobs normal guys couldn't handle or were too chicken shit to deal with."

Ben was furiously scribbling down what he was saying, trying to keep his hand steady as Rourke punched the classic Dodge to ninety.

Arnold went on. "This one time there was a guy calling himself Gorgox or Gygax or something. Claimed to be some kinda alien from Planet X and that he'd developed some kind of ray-gun that fuckin' disintegrated people. Eisenhower was pissing in his well-tailored pants when he heard about it. Sent for us right away."

Ben grinned. "A real, no bullshit ray-gun?"

"Turned out not to be. He was just...boy, Troy had a good time kicking his ass, I tell yah what. Turned out the guy was a disgruntled employee of Warner Brothers special effects department. He just threw random shit together to make it look like a gun. He dressed up like a fuckin' spaceman." Arnold laughed. "That's the thing about it. When the weirdoes started coming out of the woodwork, you had to call on the guys who were just as weird, just as tough or just as bat-shit crazy as they were."

There was silence between them except for the sound of the engine.

Arnold heaved a heavy sigh. "You know—it's a shame about Deacon. The kid was always messed up in the head but he was one of us. He was never much for ass-kicking. He never threw a punch in all the years we worked together. He let whatever that mold stuff was do all the fighting for him. Mostly he'd be the guy who got information out of people. All he had to do was touch someone and they'd sing like a canary."

Ben looked up from his notepad. "So, he wasn't violent?"

Rourke spoke up. "Unless you count the people he ate."

Arnold shook his head. "He only got that way when the alien inside of him took over. Usually, he was a blank slate. Constantly neutral. My guess is he was struggling with whatever it was he got infected with all the time. He never showed one iota of emotion… Except this one time…"

CHAPTER TEN

May. 1975.
Just outside Washington, DC.

Senator Stevenson had reached out to Parker McCoy in Washington. His daughter had gone missing while he had been busy stumping for reelection. Both the nanny and au pair both claimed ignorance, but Senator Stevenson was no fool. He knew McCoy's small group of Exceptionals— The Crimson Howl, The Automatic Man, The Swami, and Deacon James— could get him the information he needed and knew they could find his daughter for him

It didn't take long for them to show. An unmarked black Buick drove up the sprawling driveway. Stevenson felt equal parts relieved and embarrassed when four grown men in costumes stepped out of the car.

"Thank you for coming so quickly, gentlemen, Senator Stevenson greeted as the four men climbed the steps. He looked at the quartet.

The Crimson Howl wore his traditional costume of red silk and black leather, a mask, and a helmet with a wolf pelt.

The Automatic Man behind him was garbed head to toe in red and blue with a white cape draped over his broad shoulders.

The Swami—a mulatto— wore a tan tunic, a turban, and a medallion on a gold chain around his neck.

The most unsettling was the man named Deacon James in the sterile dress whites of an asylum worker; he made Stevenson's skin crawl. Deacon's expression was blank. His gaze glazed over and staring at something no one could see.

"Anything to help one of our elected officials," The Automatic Man declared. The Senator forced a weak smile.

He motioned for them to come into his home.

•••

Stevenson led the quartet to his study and explained the situation quickly. His seven-year-old daughter, Sarah, had vanished from his home. Both the nanny and the au pair had been inside the home when Sarah went missing and had already claimed innocence. While one or both were obviously lying, Stevenson couldn't prove it. The local police as well as the FBI had questioned them but neither had made any headway.

Rudyard Sinclair—The Swami— spoke after the Senator told his story. "And you want us to do what, exactly?"

"What do you mean? I want you to get them to admit they know where Sarah is!" Stevenson explained.

"And how would you like us to do that?"

Stevenson's face flashed red. "However how weirdoes get shit done!" His voice rose only slightly. He pointed his finger directly in Rudyard's face. "You know, it would be a shame if I had to tell your handlers about what you do at night. Who you spend your downtime with.

Rudyard looked at Troy who looked at Arnold. The three shared a laugh.

"Oh sugar, that's the worst kept secret in D.C." Rudyard's smile turned serious and he pointed his finger at Stevenson in return. "Let's get one thing absolutely clear, Senator. We're not Mafioso guinea thugs. We don't beat people up who don't deserve it and we certainly don't go around beating up nannies just because some rich asshole forgot how to be a parent."

Stevenson's face turned dark red. "Why you sawed-off little faggot!"

"He may be a little faggot, but he's our little faggot, Senator." Troy Berlin— The Automatic Man—grinned. "Have no fear We've got other methods of making them talk."

Senator Stevenson grunted in frustration and turned his back on them to compose himself.

There was a moment of silence. Stevenson turned around, cheeks wet with tears.

"I'm sorry," he wiped his face. "I'm used to being in control, being on top of things. The idea that my little girl is out there and that I can't do anything about it? It's killing me. And I know what kind of animals are out there. I know you've been hunting them. That's why I called for you. Please. I know one of them knows where she is—I just know it!"

"We understand, Senator." The Crimson Howl affirmed. "We'll get to the bottom of it. We'll find her."

"Take me to the man and to the woman." Deacon's voice was an eerie monotone that echoed badly in the large study. He rose from the leather chair. "I will gather the information you are seeking." He looked off into the distance, his face never changing expression.

For a moment the Senator stood there, looking at the strange man with the peach fuzz haircut and mannequin face.

"Uhm…Ri…right this way. In the kitchen." Stevenson directed.

He led the four men down a cavernous hallway into what looked like an industrial kitchen. There, sitting at a small wooden table were the two caregivers. One, was a large black woman, the other a skinny, pale man who kept his gaze on the floor.

"This is Annabelle and Pierre. They claim they know nothing about my daughter's disappearance." He narrowed his eyes in suspicion. "One of them is lying."

"I'm no liar, sir." Annabelle claimed. "I wouldn't do nothing to that little angel! Swear to Jesus" Tears rolled down her cheeks.

Pierre said nothing; his gaze remained on the floor.

Deacon sat down across from the two caregivers. His expression neutral.

Annabelle looked panicked. "What are you going to do? Please don't hurt me, sir."

"Put out your hand, please," Deacon commanded.

She did as she was told. Deacon placed his hand on hers. The panic on her face melted away and her expression was just as neutral as Deacon's. Her eyes glazed over.

"Where is the one named Sarah?" Deacon asked.

She answered in a monotone. "I do not know."

"Who took the one named Sarah?"

"I do not know."

Behind him, Senator Stevenson turned to The Crimson Howl. "How is he doing that?"

The Crimson Howl smiled. "It's complicated."

Deacon took his hand off Annabelle's. He turned slowly to the senator. "She is telling the truth. She is worried for the child called Sarah. She…cares for the child called Sarah."

Stevenson fumbled for words. "Remarkable. Annabelle, I'm sorry I accused you."

Deacon slowly turned to Pierre and put out his hand. "Give me your hand, please."

Pierre did not look at him. "No."

"I'd do what he says, frog eater," Troy threatened. "It'd be a shame if I had to break your arm in eight places."

"Easy, Troy." Rudyard cautioned. "Let Deacon work his magic. Go on, buddy."

Pierre started breathing heavily. His eyes darted from side to side. Before he could do anything, Deacon grabbed his hand with a swiftness even his costumed friends had never seen before.

The fear on Pierre's face melted away to indifference. His eyes became glassy.

"Where is the child called Sarah?" Deacon repeated the question.

"With him," Pierre replied, his accent gone, replaced with the same monotone as Deacon's.

"With whom is the child called Sarah with?"

"The bad man."

Deacon paused. He turned and looked at The Crimson Howl. Howl nodded.

"Who is the bad man?" he pushed.

"Michael Aquino."

The Senator's eyes widened in horror.

"How did the bad man Michael Aquino get the child called Sarah?"

Pierre took a very deep breath. "A friend of his contacted me after his acquittal. He had been lying low for weeks but he was hungry again. He offered me fifty thousand dollars for the child. I agreed. Stevenson doesn't pay me well enough to support my opium habit."

"There is more," Deacon added.

"I gave them the address of her school. I insisted to Annabelle that I drive her that day. Usually, she walks with Annabelle but it was raining. We arranged a pickup at nine A.M."

Pierre moved his hand, but Deacon still kept a light grip on it. Pierre unbuttoned the cuff of his shirt and rolled up his sleeve. On his forearm was a tattoo of a red pentagram with the word SET underneath. "I was a disciple of the church of Levay, as was Michael Aquino. He was thrown out for his appetites. I would not forsake him."

"Where is the child called Sarah?" Deacon repeated.

"Not far from here. Michael Aquino is hiding in the old Hill Mansion, two counties over from this one."

Deacon removed his hand from Pierre's. He looked dazed.

"We must go," Deacon told his companions. "We must save the child called Sarah."

"Not before I do something first," Troy said.

He stood Pierre up and before Pierre could protest what was happening, got a dose of The Automatic Man's fist in his face. The Frenchman's teeth skittered across the tile floor. Blood oozed from his gums. Troy looked down at the whimpering heap on the floor. "You're lucky I held back, you white-flag-waving fuck!" He kicked the man in the stomach with such force he slid halfway across the kitchen.

"Let's go," Troy turned to the others. "Before it's too late. This Aquino guy is an animal and hunting season just opened."

•••

They drove in silence. It would take them forty minutes to get to the old Hill Mansion. Howl glanced over at Troy and watched the rage wash over him. Troy had become the father of twin girls not even a week ago. This was going to get messy.

•••

These types of cases were always hard. It was the reason Arnold kept a bottle of Old Grandad in the glove compartment of the Buick. When the victims of these lunatics were children, it always hit them harder than they cared to admit. The Crimson Howl would be going away for a while later that night and it would just be Arnold Grant getting well and truly drunk with whatever booze it took for as long as it took.

Provided, of course, they weren't too late.

The papers only wrote about their successes. Parker McCoy had a few people working for the newspapers in D.C. who glossed over their failures. Despite what the Washington Post wrote, they sometimes didn't make it in time. A kid got chopped to bits, or a starlet was gang raped by some weirdo sex cult but the people never knew about those things. If the tide of public opinion was to ever turn against superheroes . . .

"Can't this shitbox go any faster?" Troy bitched.

"Giving it all the gas I can." The Crimson Howl replied. "Rudy, when we get there, I'm gonna need you to put that medallion to work

Rudyard nodded. "You got it."

The Crimson Howl looked over at Deacon. "Deacon, if you find the girl, get her out of the house. Do you understand?"

Deacon stared out the window, his expression blank.

Howl cleared his throat, "I said if you find…"

"Deacon will do what Arnold Grant says. When Deacon finds the child named Sarah, Deacon will get her out of the house."

An uncomfortable moment passed between them all.

"Uh…good." The Crimson Howl pulled up to a long driveway. Ivy had overgrown the wrought-iron gate but thankfully it was open (and had been for years.) The asphalt was cracked and littered with potholes. At the top of the steep driveway was the Hill Mansion. The windows had been shuttered and a few of them had been boarded up. Weeds had overgrown the shrubbery that surrounded the house.

The men got out of the car and huddled near the back.

"Okay, Rudy." Howl took charge. "Put on that medallion and make us invisible."

Rudyard didn't move. "You know I love you, big guy, but it only works on me."

The Crimson Howl grimaced. "Shit. Well, then you're gonna go in first. Troy, think you can get in without rousing any suspicion?"

Troy grinned. "I'll be in the house before Rudy can say abra cadabra."

Howl nodded.

"What about Deacon and Arnold Grant?" Deacon was staring at the house, or maybe looking through it.

Howl reconsidered. "We'll go around to the far end of the yard and see if we can't slip in through one of the windows on the first floor. Be quick, Deacon. This ain't no time for goldbrickin'"

"When this is over you must explain to Deacon what it means to gold brick."

Howl raised an eyebrow. He was pretty sure that was Deacon's attempt at levity. "Ready?"

Troy and Rudyard were set to go.

Rudyard pulled the Medallion of Delphi from a pocket in his tunic and put it on. It cast a warm purple glow. Rudyard closed his eyes and mouthed a few words to himself, gesticulating with both hands.

In a blink he was gone. Invisible. The only proof of his existence was the sound of his soft-soled shoes hitting the cracked driveway.

By the time Howl and Deacon were halfway up the driveway, Troy had made it to the front door. He was joined by Rudyard who rematerialized next to him.

"Man, you're fast." Rudyard whispered.

"So do we knock?" Troy's voice was barely a whisper

Rudyard rubbed his smooth, tan chin. "Before you go off on a beating spree, let me find the girl." He put his hand on the doorknob. It wouldn't turn. "Figured it'd be locked. No matter." He closed his eyes again and muttered a few words. On the other side of the door, the faint sound of a bolt snapping was heard.

The door opened slightly.

•••

The foyer of the Hill Mansion was just as dilapidated and worn out as the outside driveway and lawn. A collapsed staircase greeted Rudyard and Troy as they entered. Broken glass and empty beer and liquor bottles littered the floor. Spray-painted on the torn-up wallpaper were some ugly graffiti tags and initials. To the right of the foyer was a sitting area; a couch, too modern to have been the original furniture, lay about ten feet away from the large picture window which has been boarded up. The fireplace had recently been used. The house smelled like mold and stale booze and the skunky smell of reefer.

The Swami's vision was clouded by the power of the Medallion of Delphi. He saw the house as it used to be, grand and ornate. The staircase was intact and at the top stood a little girl. She couldn't have been more than seven or eight. Her eyes were brown saucers, matching the color of her hair. Rudyard could see her face was wet with tears.

"You are not Sarah…but you died here recently."

The little girl looked down with a mixed look of terror and amazement. "You…you can see me?"

The Swami smiled, "Yes, child. The Swami sees all and knows much." It was a line he liked to use when talking to the dead. Sometimes they could be a bit…difficult.

The little girl walked to the edge of the staircase and took a step but found she couldn't.

"Why can't I leave?"

"Because you died there." The Swami said, matter-of-factly.

"I want my mommy," The girl pleaded. "The bad man…he…he put his…"

The Swami waved his hand. "Hush, child. I know what he did to you. I know how he killed you. How he hurts children. I'm here to stop him from hurting someone else. Can you help me?"

The little girl nodded.

"Good. You know there is a girl here."

"Yes. I can't see her though. She isn't up here and I can't come down."

"Is she hurt? Has he…?"

The spirit-girl shook her head. "He's not ready for her yet. He has to say his prayers first. Like he did before with me."

Rudyard shuddered at the thought. "Where is she?"

The girl pointed to the right. "In the kitchen. There's a big closet there. She's in it. That's where he kept me before he…"

"Where is the bad man?"

The girl closed her eyes tight. "The cellar. It's a bad place."

The Swami smiled warmly. "Thank you."

"Mister?" The girl said, her voice gone soft. "I don't wanna stay here anymore. I'm scared. I want my mommy and daddy." Her voice trailed off to a whimper. She was crying again.

Rudyard knew he was running out of time but didn't care. It was bad enough the Senator's daughter was here, worse still was that this poor thing had been raped and murdered and no one knew. He knew what he had to do. He ascended the spectral stairs quickly and took the spirit girl's hands in his. The spirit girl's hands were ethereal, like holding fog.

The Medallion of Delphi's light changed from blue-green to yellow.

The Swami smiled at the girl. "I release you from this place of torment. Go and be at peace."

The light emanating from the Medallion grew brighter, and stronger. The hairs on the back of Rudyards's neck prickled. Behind the girl, a swirling vortex of blue-white light formed. She turned and looked at Rudyard, unsure of what to do.

"Be at peace." His voice creaked. This happened sometimes when he sent the ghosts away. He smiled despite the tears. "Go on."

The spirit did as she was told and disappeared into the void. The blue and white vortex faded as the Medallion's light changed from yellow to blue-green.

Rudyard turned to walk down the spectral stairs but stopped.

At the foot of the stairs was a man with a gun.

"Stay where you are or I'll …" Before the would-be gunman could finish, Troy snuck up on him with total silence and snapped his neck. The gunman fell to the ground with a thud.

Rudyard sighed in relief. "Thanks."

Troy smiled, "Sure thing, buddy." He glared at the dead man lying on the rotting floor.

"Was that him?" Rudyard quickly and quietly ran down the ethereal steps.

"No. But I know this piece of shit. His name is Hambright. Son of a bitch is a Baptist minister."

"Was." Rudyard leaned in over the body, which had just expelled its bodily fluids, and spat on it.

From behind, The Crimson Howl heaved a sigh. "Why don't you two idiots

"The cellar. It's a bad place."

make some more noise?"

Rudyard turned to Deacon. "The girl is safe. She's in a closet in the kitchen. Find her and get her to the car."

"Deacon will do this." He walked off.

Howl crouched and examined the body. "Is this him?"

"An accomplice," Troy replied.

Rudyard nodded. "Our guy is in the cellar. The girl is unhurt."

The Crimson Howl grunted, "How do you know?"

Rudyard smiled and patted his pocket. "The Medallion knows much. Let's go."

CHAPTER ELEVEN

The Crimson Howl could smell the blood from the top of the stairs. The blunt metallic scent mixed with the smell of long rotten vegetables, mold, and the raw, base smell of semen nearly made him gag.

He could hear a deep, commanding voice speaking a foreign language. Latin, he guessed.

"Guys," Howl whispered, "I got a feeling we ain't gonna like what we see down there."

Troy grinned. There was bloodlust in his eyes.

Howl didn't like it.

"Only one way to find out." Troy opened the door slowly. Luckily for them, it didn't squeak or groan. The voice went on with its strange, foreign chanting. They descended the stairs into the cellar.

The Crimson Howl was right.

The cellar was sparse. The floor was mostly dirt. A few mushrooms sprung from the floor in the darker corners of the room. Candles of every size gave off a dim light. A makeshift altar had been assembled on a wooden board in the far left corner where the chanting man stood. Across from the altar, a raw, skinned goat's head was mounted on a pike; maggots pulsated through its orifices as giant horseflies circled it. The walls were speckled with blood. It was fresh blood, The Crimson Howl noticed.

On the ceiling, supported by the crossbeams were hooks. The type a person could find in a meat packing plant. Hanging from one of them, with the blunt metal sticking out through her chest was a girl no older than seven, with brown hair and brown eyes. Her eyes were wide open, a look of pain forever etched on her face. Her neck was bruised. A sure sign she had been strangled. Howl didn't have to look further down to know what else had happened to her.

He could smell it.

"Dear God!" Rudyard gasped in revulsion. His hand went to his mouth in disgust and horror.

The chanting suddenly stopped and the bad man, Michael Aquino, turned to face them. He was clothed in a black robe. Slowly, he turned the hood down, revealing his face.

Howl noticed he was pale and portly, not the type of person you'd associate with devil worship. Hell, he looked downright grandfatherly. His hair was white on the top and gray on the sides. He raised a tufted eyebrow at the trio.

"Oh. The superheroes. Come no further." He reached into his pocket.

Troy was about to rush him but Howl held up his hand.

Aquino pulled out a handful of white powder and sprinkled it at his feet. "I'm now protected from any and all threats. If you've come to make trouble, you're wasting your time."

"We've come to take you in, General," Howl stated. "You have to answer for your crimes, for what you've done lately."

"For what you did to her." Rudyard pointed to the dead girl hanging from the meat hook.

Aquino shrugged, "If you saw where I plucked her from, you'd think hanging from a meat hook was a fucking mercy. Besides, she was a crier. I hate it when they cry. She cried so fucking much I had to strangle the air right out of her."

"Bastard!" Rudyard growled and sprang towards Aquino but was held back by The Crimson Howl.

Aquino threw his head back and laughed. "Oh, now for the comic book theatrics!" He wiped a tear from his eyes with the sleeve of his robe. "You know, maybe instead of going around beating up petty criminals in those fruity fetish costumes you should pick up a law book."

Howl looked at Rudyard. The Swami had composed himself.

"That scrawny fuck Stevenson tried to throw me in jail but the prosecutor couldn't prove I gave those kids V.D. I'll show him. I'll send his daughter to him in pieces after I've had my fun."

Howl clenched his fists. "Look, for your own good, I'm beggin' ya to come with us quietly. We know the Senator's daughter is unharmed."

"No. I have powers of my own! No harm can come to me. I'm not afraid of The Crimson Howl, The Swami, or... the Human Bullet." Aquino faced Troy directly. "Say, what does your wife think of that nickname? One quick pop and it's all over?"

Rudyard looked at Arnold. They both smiled and took a step back. They didn't want to be in splatter range of the late General Aquino.

"Rudy," Troy pointed to the floor. "That shit he threw on the ground?"

"What about it?"

"Is it full of pagan hocus pocus?"

Rudyard chuckled. "No. Much like the rest of the half-assed mish-mash of nonsense he's playing at down here, it's complete bullshit."

The Crimson Howl sniffed. "Smells like talcum powder to me."

Troy flashed a toothy grin. "Good."

Suddenly General Michael Aquino didn't look so smug as the first kick to the balls connected. In fact, his pale cheeks turned a dark shade of green. Before Aquino had a chance to cry out or vomit Troy's fist connected with his nose, obliterating it. He fell hard to the ground, still conscious.

"Pppleaassse!" He managed through a mouthful of blood, "dd…dddooont!"

"Oh!" Troy kicked the former general in the balls again. "Not so fucking TOUGH when it's someone who can defend themselves!" He knelt on Aquino's chest and started punching wildly. "Fuckin' squeal, you child-raping piece of shit! That's right, take your fuckin' medicine!" Troy's face was as red as the blood pouring from Aquino's mouth. Spittle flew from Troy's mouth. "Come on ya fuckin' cocksuckin' bastard! I said SQUEAL!"

Aquino did just that. It was a pitiful, high-pitched yell. He screamed until his lungs gave out and his heart burst under Troy's hammering fists. In a last bit of fury, Troy got up and thrust Aquino's lifeless body on one of the meat hooks. He looked upon his work, his justice, and smiled. He was out of breath and sweating. He turned to Arnold and Rudyard.

"You okay now, Troy?" Arnold asked, "You got anything else you wanna get outta your system?"

"Nah," He answered panting. "Get the girl. We aren't leaving her here with this piece of shit." Then he pointed to the corpse of the dead girl. "Give me your cape, Howl."

Arnold undid the snaps that held his cape in place and handed it over to Troy. Troy placed it on the floor.

With tenderness he rarely showed anyone except for his wife, Troy lifted the child off the hook, as if to do otherwise would hurt the dead girl.

"I'm going to go check on Deacon," Rudyard said. "I'll meet you outside."

"Good." Howl never took his eyes off Troy as he gently placed the girl on the cape and folded her arms across her chest. Despite the smell, Troy leaned in brushed the hair from her face, and kissed her forehead. He made the sign of the Cross and covered her with the other half of the cape.

•••

Deacon didn't have to try hard to find the girl. He could hear her weeping. It was an odd sound. The cry of a human child was foreign to him. He couldn't remember if he ever cried as a child. The alien in his blood had blocked a great deal of his early memories. Now it just told him things. Sometimes they were good things and sometimes they were bad. He dared not tell his friends about how he sometimes wanted to tear them apart and eat their innards. No, he dared not say that or else he'd be sent back to the Brattleboro Asylum, only this time as a resident instead of a worker.

No walls can hold you, the alien, which had so long ago given him his incredible abilities, said in his head.

Deacon knew it was true. The mold—which was what the alien likened itself to— gave him powers. Made him smart and strong. Something he'd never be without it, but it came with a price. A bargain he'd been putting off for a while, an urge he was constantly fighting in his mind. The mold was hungry and demanded human meat in return for the amazing abilities it imbued to Deacon James.

The girl's crying came louder now. Deacon walked slowly over to the closet.

Give me the human child to eat. She is small and will not be noticed. You could tell the others you found her like this.

His normally blank face suddenly twisted into a sick grimace. Yes, the girl wouldn't be missed. He could make very short work of her. Her guts would be easy to eat and . . .

"No!" He whispered, his voice full of anger and betrayal. "You stop it right now! Deacon won't do it!"

Deacon owes me. Deacon would still be a blithering idiot working at a crazy house if it weren't for me! Eat the girl! We'll be even then! I hunger!

Deacon's eyes welled with tears. He knew sooner or later he would have to indulge the voice in his head; he would have to scratch the itch.

"No. Next time. Please!" He whispered through the tears, "Next time I'll feed you. Just not now!"

The voice said nothing. Deacon's expression turned blank again. A victory. For now.

"Hello?" The Senator's daughter said, meekly.

Deacon opened the door slowly. Sarah was sitting on the floor, Indian style. Her little wrist was handcuffed to an exposed metal pipe. Deacon looked at the handcuff with benign puzzlement. He took the end of the cuff attached to the pipe and snapped it in half with a flick of the wrist. He got down in his knees and took her hand.

Sarah recoiled from his touch. "Are...are you gonna hurt me?"

He looked at the girl, his expression ever neutral. "No. We have come to rescue the child named Sarah." He sensed mistrust from the girl. He didn't exactly have a face you could trust. He held out his hand. "Come with me, please."

She shook her head. "You're scary. Like the bad man."

You see? She thinks you're a monster. Prove her right and FEED. ME.

"No." he answered, barely audible, "Deacon will not hurt you, child na… Sarah. Deacon was sent by your father to find you. To bring you home."

"You talk funny," Sarah noticed.

"Deacon does not talk funny." He looked genuinely perplexed. His blank expression must have changed because suddenly the girl giggled.

"Do too."

"Deacon does not," his tone slightly defensive.

The girl giggled again. It finally dawned on Deacon James that the girl was becoming less afraid of him. He held out his hand again.

"Will you come with me? The man who talks funny?" He was neutral again. If he was grateful that Sarah finally took his outstretched hand, he didn't show it. He took the girl in his arms, picked her up, and walked out of the kitchen and into the dilapidated living room. Sarah hugged Deacon tightly, her breath warm against his neck.

Suddenly there was a screaming coming from the cellar. It was a high-pitched screech. Sarah screamed and dug her little nails into Deacon's neck. He didn't see the beer can and tripped on it, falling to his knees.

Sarah began crying again.

He looked at her, perplexed. The screams were getting louder and louder. The girl was terrified. She buried her face in his shoulder. Deacon wanted to comfort her. He wondered briefly how his mother used to comfort him when he cried or was scared. He couldn't remember. The mold wouldn't let him sometimes.

He tried and struggled to remember. The mold wasn't right about him. He wasn't a monster. A monster didn't have friends and save little girls from bad men. A monster didn't do those things.

A hero did.

And a hero knew how to comfort a little girl when she was terrified.

Suddenly, thankfully, he got a glimpse. His mother, stroking his hair and… singing.

That gave Deacon a warm feeling in his stomach.

He stroked Sarah's hair and began to sing. An old song he was fond of when he didn't have powers.

Blue skies smiling at me
Nothing but blue skies

Do I see.

His voice faltered a bit. It had been years since he used to mop the piss and shit off the asylum floors singing that song until one of his coworkers would push him and tell him to stop. As the screams down in the cellar grew louder and more strained, his voice grew stronger. He gently stroked Sarah's hair. Her sobbing slows down to whimpers.

He continued.

Blue Birds
Singing a song
Nothing but blue birds
all day long.

The screams stopped, but Deacon kept singing. The girl had fallen asleep in his arms.

Rudyard didn't approach him until he had finished. He'd later remark that he'd never heard such a sweet voice coming out of anyone before in his life.

"Shh," Deacon said. "The child named Sarah is asleep."

"Right. Come on. We're finished here," Rudyard said.

Deacon stood up slowly, Sarah's arms still hung around Deacon's neck. He followed Rudyard out the door and down the driveway; clouds had given way to a warm late spring sun. The two men got in the Buick and waited for Arnold and Troy.

•••

Troy placed the corpse of the girl in the Buick's trunk.

Arnold got in the car and started the engine. He reached over to the glove box and pulled out the bottle of Old Grandad. He gestured to Rudyard, who waved it off.

"Troy?" Arnold offered the bottle.

Troy took it and was about to take a belt but thought better of it. "Not this time."

He didn't bother offering it to Deacon. Deacon never drank. He capped the bottle, slid it under the seat, and put the car in drive. It wouldn't be long until Sarah was back home with her mom and dad. The little girl in the trunk could be laid to rest properly.

Despite the severity of what they had just been through, Arnold could tell they were proud. Proud of the justice they'd done there. Each of them had done something heroic. They'd earned their bucktails that day.

They were silent the entire ride back to the Senator's estate. It was a good silence. The silence of a job well done. They wouldn't swap this story with any of the other Exceptionals. This was one they'd keep between them.

Arnold glanced over at the little girl who was sleeping comfortably in Deacon's arms. Then, a sight that gave Arnold pause.

Deacon staring out the window at nothing. Smiling.

Deacon James was smiling.

Despite the death they saw that day, despite the horror, Arnold smiled too.

CHAPTER TWELVE

Ben looked at Arnold with both awe and admiration. He'd been taking notes for the past hour, enraptured.

"Sad part was, a few weeks later he started eating people," Arnold related. "We figured that day with that little girl might have made him a little bit more human, you know?"

"How come none of this was in our files?" Ben asked. "You certainly didn't put it in your book."

"It was private. We asked Parker not to run it in the papers. I figured there are some things better left unsaid in that book of mine. Christ a'mighty, I don't think I ever felt more like a hero than I did that day, and I barely did a goddamed thing."

Rourke once again found himself hanging on Arnold's every word in spite of himself. "So, what did they do after that? What happened to the Hill Mansion?"

"They bulldozed the fucker with that kiddiddlin' bastard still in the cellar. Last I heard the land was sold and they turned it into an industrial park."

"And I guess the government covered up the whole thing, seeing as he was a general and all."

"I don't know much about that, I'm sure his records and files have been redacted all to hell. Fact of the matter is, we all learned something that day. I mean, we dealt with psychopaths before. It was our fuckin' job, but that day was…it was a turning point for us."

"How so?" Ben stopped writing.

Arnold was quiet for several moments. "Things just felt different. Deacon started chomping on people and the Act was repealed and all that." He shook his head. "Soon no one put on the cape anymore and that was that."

Rourke snickered. "Fuckin' government ruins everything."

He was surprised that Arnold laughed too.

"Fuckin'-A." Arnold looked back at Ben. "You can put that in your notes."

They stopped for gas a short time later. Rourke had volunteered to keep driving but the giant truckstop breakfast was sitting heavy. No amount of coffee was going to keep him awake. Ben, who seemed to be relishing the prospect of mining Arnold for more stories, was more than happy to drive another few hours. They switched seats and were on the road again.

In the back, Rourke had settled in as best he could, removing his shoes bunching his long coat into a ball, and lying down across the back. It wasn't the most comfortable position, but he figured he should at least try to get some sleep if he wanted to drive later on. He tried to let the hum of the engine and the road lull him to sleep. No easy feat when you were bent in half in the backseat of a car.

"Better not drool on the leather, pipsqueak," Arnold warned.

Rourke was surprised at his tone. It seemed to be only half-serious.

Rourke didn't retort. He couldn't think of anything witty to say anyway. He closed his eyes, hoping he'd fall asleep soon.

It took him about an hour before he finally dozed off into a surprisingly deep sleep.

The road spread forward in its hypnotic way as the sky went from peach to purple. There was a long silence between Ben and Arnold. A silence bred not from lack of anything to say but one that comes from being on the road for hours.

"So, what's the deal with pipsqueak back there?" Arnold's voice a little too loud for Ben's liking. He had gotten used to the silence.

"What do you mean?"

"He seems a little high strung, don't you think?"

"Rourke used to really love this job. Hell, almost as much as I do. In his own way of course."

A tiny snort from The Crimson Howl. "And you're practically creaming your jeans whenever I tell a story. So what happened to him? Guy seems to have it out for me."

"He doesn't have it out for you. He just doesn't like you."

This brought a guffaw.

"Now I know that, Irish, but why? What's he got against little old me?"

"Nothing in particular. He just has a thing about Exceptional people. They bother him."

"That ain't no explanation, Irish," Howl pointed out. "In my line a'work, a man has to have a reason for hatin' another man. What happened? Some geriatric supervillain kill his girlfriend or something?"

"Rourke had a wife once."

"Did she leave him because he had a stick jammed so far up his ass, she got splinters when he kissed her?"

"Nah, nothin' like that. They met when we were sophomores at B.U. She was studying nursing. The three of us hung out a lot. Became basically inseparable like Harry, Ron, and Hermione."

"Who?"

Ben sighed. "The Three Musketeers."

"Ah. I understood that reference. So, what happened? She left him for someone who used to wear a cape?"

"She died."

There was a pause. Arnold let out a grunt of understanding. "So lemme guess. A supervillain or some criminal scumbag killed her?"

"You could say that."

Arnold raised an eyebrow. "Really? Who?"

"The Big C."

Arnold's brow furrowed, "Never heard of him."

Another pause, this time Ben broke the silence. "Cancer. Pancreatic. Found out when it was too late for the doctors to do anything about it. A month after she found diagnosed, she was in hospice. Two weeks after that, she was dead."

Arnold sighed. "Christ."

"Rourke was...well, devastated isn't the word, and he told me when he finally came back to work that if there are guys with powers, honest to God powers, why couldn't they do anything to save his wife? If guys like Parker McCoy- with his tremendous intellect could turn regular guys like you into Exceptionals, why couldn't he cure cancer? He wasn't the same after that."

There was silence between them for the next hour.

•••

Arnold Grant took the driver's seat at their last gas stop. Rourke sat in the front and Ben was in the back, sleeping soundly.

Arnold glanced over at the thin, brown-haired Special Agent who had taken such a dislike to him and found himself thinking of long ago when he was Rourke's age and all he'd accomplished by then. He noticed a few similarities between him and the kid. They both started out loving what they did but tragedy had taken away their zeal.

"I knew a girl once," Arnold declared and the words hung in the air for a long time.

"What?"

"I said I knew a girl once. It was back in the late sixties." Arnold rubbed the stubble on his chin. "We were on different sides of a very important mission."

Rourke arched an eyebrow. "You sure you wanna tell me this? I can't write as fast as Ben."

"Yeah, I wanna tell ya. You can just rehash it to Irish when he wakes up if you think he need to hear it. He's a good kid, maybe he don't need to hear about this." Arnold kept his eyes on the road. "We were asked by our handlers in Washington to deal with some militant Negroes who were burning down Newark. It was a short time after Martin Luther King got killed."

Rourke rolled his eyes. "Let me guess, you guys had something to do with that?"

"Hell no! And before ya' get any other stupid ideas, we didn't kill Kennedy either. Fuckin' comedian, you are."

"Take it easy. Go on."

Arnold was slightly hurt. "I voted for Jack Kennedy and I actually liked that King fella's message. Unfortunately, it didn't jive with the jackboots in Washington and we were on the payroll so when they told us to go to Newark to crack some skulls, we did. Anyway, there was a group that was affiliated with the Black Panther Party. You heard of them, right?"

Rourke nodded.

"We'd made our way there it was all fire and blood. People were throwing bricks and Molotov's, just tearin' the fuckin' place apart. These were some angry people, and to be honest, with the exception of Troy, Rudy and I had our doubts about even being there."

"You had a problem with beating on angry black kids? I find that highly unlikely."

"Well, those heads had to be broke. They were burnin' down their own neighborhoods. They needed to be reminded of that. I said we had doubts, I didn't say what we did was wrong."

"You could make the argument, though. Especially in light of all the shit Ehrlichman admitted. Hell, who knows how much of that shit was started by government plants? Regardless, where's this story going?"

"I'm getting to the point, that is, if you wouldn't interrupt me with the Ivory Tower interjections. So, we'd come across this group that was affiliated with the Black Panthers. We figured we'd be in and out of Newark. Beat up a few shines and be back in Washington before you could say race riot. But this group, we underestimated their leader. She was one of the toughest women I ever knew," the old hero was smiling at the recollection.

"She?"

"Isabella Elizabeth-Jones; also known as Lady Panther. She was one of the toughest fighters I'd ever seen. Made us retreat a couple of times. None of us were sure if she was an Exceptional or just a really well-trained martial artist, but damn. She used that ching-chang kung fooey like one of them guys in those badly dubbed chink movies." Arnold laughed. "I ain't ashamed to admit she kicked my ass in broad daylight. Thankfully it was in an alley where no one saw. Threw me in a fuckin' dumpster. Said I was white trash, so I might as well be white trash."

"So what happened? Troy probably got a hold of her and snapped her neck."

"No. Troy was busy dealing with some of the other members of her gang. Rudy, too. Lots of times when we tussled it was just me and her. That's how this shit starts. You're going back and forth, beating the hell out of each other, exchanging verbal barbs and the next thing you know, the two of you are fuckin' in the back alley while the city is burning down all around you."

Rourke grimaced. "Could've done without the mental image."

"Heh, kid if you saw what Isabella looked like in that tight shirt and camo pants, I don't think your pecker would be able to handle it."

"Charming,"

Arnold paused for a moment, "We didn't think it was going to take a month to quell the riots. Like I said, we underestimated the resolve of these people. Isabella and I, well, we decided we liked each other a lot. Next thing I knew, I found myself helping her out."

"Troy must have been thrilled."

Arnold shot a look at Rourke, "I never told him about that but I think he pieced it together. Best you don't say anything to him about it. I think he's still sore over it."

Rourke made a gesture with his hand zipping his lips together.

"It was a different time back then, kid," Arnold continued. "Blacks and whites really hated each other. You think it's bad now? Shit, back then if a white girl and a black guy were found together that old Joe got his balls cut off. I ain't even exaggerating."

"I hope you survived intact."

"Now, I ain't got nothin' against the Negroes, but they are savages when it comes to their women. I guess someone found out about us. We were supposed to meet on the roof of an abandoned building, as Superheroes often do, but she was late for the rendezvous. After an hour of waiting around for her, I decide to leave. I'm climbing down the fire escape when I see this Cadillac pull up to the alley. Next thing I know two shines are pullin' Isabella out of the car, bare-ass naked. I was too high up to jump down, a fall from that distance woulda' crippled me."

Rourke looked at Arnold. "They killed her?"

"They'd shot her about forty times, and that was after somebody had broken everyone bone in her body. They spit on her corpse, sayin' she was a traitor to her race. Left her in the alley among the trash and filth. Fuckin' nigg..."

He stopped himself from finishing the word. "Sorry, I'm from a different generation."

"It's okay. Just be glad Ben isn't awake or I'd have to break your jaw."

"It ain't okay. See up till then, I used to love my job. Throwin' on the cape and the mask was my whole life up till that point. When she got killed..." He trailed off. "Those fuckin apes shot her in the face. She had such a pretty face."

Rourke could only muster, "I'm sorry."

"Worst part was, I was never able to figure out who did it. We broke the Panthers, hell, we broke everybody. We made them confess to all sorts of shit by the time Troy was finished. Washington didn't want to take no chances. But nobody ever 'fessed up to why they killed her." Arnold cleared his throat. "I almost hung up the costume after that."

"You became disillusioned. I know the feeling."

Arnold smiled weakly. "I bet, kid."

CHAPTER THIRTEEN

The sun was sinking and the sky had turned purple and the air finally stopped feeling so damned oppressive. Ben had rolled down his window, letting an arm hang outside. He flexed his hand, his wrist cramping from the previous hours of writing. Rourke dropped back off to sleep and, without an audience, Howl just stared out the window.

It had been desert sand outside for most of the trip. A few cacti and a lonely buzzard picking at an unlucky coyote were the highlights. However, as they passed through Roswell, Ben had expected the normalcy of a city. Instead, there were tourist traps and weird signs about alien encounters stuck in random yards. Grey or green heads with large oval eyes watched them pass from fast food joints and grocery chains. Arnold grinned when he saw these things while Rourke, Ben guessed, rolled his eyes in his sleep.

"If these people really knew what happened that day in '47, boy," Arnold uttered. Ben was hoping he'd elaborate, but Arnold just laughed softly and went back to staring out the window. The rest of the city passed quickly as Ben took the expressway north out of town. Another forty minutes later, they got off on County Road 20, and followed it into the desert.

"Hey Irish. Up ahead, take a left," Arnold directed.

"You sure? Doesn't look like much more than a hiking trail."

"Don't argue kid. Just make the turn,"

Ben did as he was told, trying to keep the old hero's car on the narrow path. A handful of minutes later, Arnold spoke again, "Kill it Irish." As the car came to a stop, Rourke sat up groggily, rubbing his eyes. Arnold was silent. He took a deep breath and began to speak.

"We're about to visit Troy Berlin in his own home. He doesn't like visitors, even ones he's expecting. Troy is funny that way. He's funny in a lot of ways and if you piss him off, you're gonna find out why they call him the Automatic Man. Now, I can't guarantee your safety, but I can vouch for you. If I say you're both stand-up guys, he's apt to believe me on the basis of our very long friendship. Still, even if you follow the rules, a look, a gesture, a word he doesn't like or misconstrues may lead to bodily harm or a bloody death."

Rourke opened his mouth to comment, but the tone of Arnold's voice stopped him. It wasn't exactly fear, but it more than anxiety. He'd been in interrogations and watched the truth sweat out of people. Arnold was telling the truth, or most of it, but he was antsy about something and Rourke didn't like it.

Arnold elaborated. "The first rule is to smile. Keep things light and don't look too uncomfortable. He'll take it as an insult. Second rule is to compliment his wife, Vera. She's an old Southern Belle and flattery works best on her. Flatter but don't flirt. Last guy who did that was a traveling salesman who got his jaw busted so bad the doctors couldn't salvage it. If she offers you anything to eat or drink, you take it. I don't care if it's cat piss with a side of dog turds wrapped in bacon. You take it, eat it, drink it, tell her it's the best you ever had, and smile wide. Third rule is do not talk about Troy's daughters unless Troy directly mentions them to you. They are his pride and joy but they're different so don't stare. You stare and you're a dead man. Do either of you need me to repeat any of these rules to you?"

Both men shook their heads.

"Okay," Arnold said, "Let's go. We're burnin' daylight. In a half a mile make a right. His house is a mile and a half up the road from there."

The trail ahead remained barren, and in the growing dusk, Ben saw stars emerging in the night sky like diamond pinpricks. Secluded? This wasn't secluded. It was desolate like he imagined the moon would be. The Dodge crested a small hill and Ben saw the dim lights of a house in the distance. It was the only light as far as he could see that didn't live in the sky.

As they got closer to the house, the dirt road became gravel. The driveway was long, almost as long as Arnold's, but lacking the extravagant gates and well-manicured hedges. Instead, the desert sand gave way to a rich green lawn bordered by a white picket fence.

"It's Astroturf," Arnold said. "Troy never could get grass to grow out here."

"Does that have anything to do with the nuclear tests?" Rourke questioned.

"I think so. That and it's the fuckin' desert." He smirked, but Rourke didn't see it.

4

The driveway was long...

Ben stopped the car in the driveway. Instead of a garage, there was a carport. Under the awning was a vintage 1980 Ford LTD Country Squire, avocado green with faux wood trim. The New Mexico license plate said ATM1938.

"The Automatic Man drives a station wagon," Rourke said in disbelief.

Arnold turned to Rourke. "He's got kids."

Then he opened the door. "Follow me, but not too close. Give me some space while I ring the bell."

Ben pointed his finger at Rourke. "You better keep that fool mouth of yours shut."

Rourke showed an expression of mock offense. "I'll be on my best behavior, boss."

"You damned well better be, boyo," Ben warned. "I don't know about you but I don't wanna fuckin' die in New Mexico."

Rourke nodded. They waited at the bottom of the porch steps as Arnold ascended.

The porch was littered with toys. Sand pails and shovels, a couple of old dolls with patchy hair and limbs missing, two pink tricycles, one overturned, another with a broken pedal. The paint on the steps was peeling and a broken wind chime tried in vain to sing. The porch light gave off a low wattage golden glow that barely illuminated the steps.

Arnold rang the bell and put on his best smile. He glanced back at the Rourke and Ben.

"Smile, fellas."

Rourke heard the pitter patter of tiny feet scurry around. A tiny girl broadcasted to the others in the house that she would get it. Another, much smaller voice said that no, she would get it. A second pitter patter of feet drummed through the house. The two tiny voices joined in as one and declared they would both get it and dissolved into a fit of giggles.

The door swung open and both Rourke and Ben were taken slightly aback by what they saw.

Rourke had seen midgets (little people, Jillian had said once), mostly on television but this didn't look like common dwarfism. The girls were small, sure. Maybe only three and a half feet tall, but their heads were oddly shaped, more oval than round. Their eye sockets appeared much larger than normal. The girl on the right had one green eye and one purple eye, while the girl on the left had an albino red eye and a hazel one. Both sets of eyes shone, even in the dim light. Their limbs were impossibly small, almost bony. The girl on the right had blonde hair so fine it looked like it could fall out if touched. The other girl's hair was half white and half light brown. Her skin was irregular too. It was blotchy on one side but extremely pale on the other side of her face with a red eye and white hair. The girl on the right had skin so thin it was almost translucent. Rourke could see nearly every blue-green vein in her head and the massive vein near her tiny temple pulsed notably.

The girls grinned, revealing mouthfuls of baby teeth with one or two adult ones.

"Uncle Arnold!" they squealed in unison.

Arnold got down low, the grin on his face reaching from ear to ear. "Hiya girls!" He enveloped them in a gentle hug. The two children squealed even louder. "Is mama home?"

"She's always home!" The girl on the left, the half-albino, said. "Mama!"

From behind them a woman's voice called. "Just a second, Maude, baby. You and Bernadette had better not be talking to strangers!"

In unison, the girls answered, "We aren't," then giggled mischievously. The two little girls scurried into the kitchen like a pair of odd mice.

Vera Berlin materialized in the doorway, her hair in a beehive. She was wearing a white sundress with red polka dots and an apron, an oven-mitt on her right hand, and a spatula in the other. She looked very much the quintessential 50's housewife except for her face.

To Ben, Vera looked as if her face was made entirely out of plastic like she'd had work done and then had it shellacked to preserve it. Her face had no wrinkles and was pulled back so tight her mouth was constantly grinning, even if she wasn't actively smiling. Her lips, artificially plump and slathered with red lipstick glinted in the soft glow. She was slender, with rounded hips giving her a classic hourglass figure. Ben's experience at reading faces for emotion wasn't helping him much here but at least her tone suggested she was delighted to see them.

"Arnold Grant, as I live and breathe!" she declared in a way that reminded Rourke of Vivien Leigh in Gone With the Wind. She hurried from the kitchen through the alcove to the three smiling men standing in her doorway. A delirious sense that they had been transported into some slasher movie came over Ben.

"Vera, you look just as pretty as the last time I saw you!" Arnold complimented. If he was lying, Ben couldn't tell. Arnold embraced her, even lifting her up in the air a little. She laughed with delight.

"Oh, you do go awon, Mistah Grahyant," her drawl thickening. Vera leaned back to look at him. "Oh, Arnold, you look terrible."

Arnold grinned. "California will do that to you."

Vera frowned. At least Rourke thought she did. It was very difficult to tell.

"The day California sinks into the ocean will be a good day. A regular Sodom, if you ask me." She paused. "Oh, where are my manners, get out of that doorway, and come sit down!" She led them to an upholstered couch that looked older than Rourke and Ben combined.

"Troy will be down in a minute. He's washing up for supper. Oh, gee, where are my manners!?" She looked at Rourke and Ben, "Vera Berlin. Lady of the house."

Ben was the first to introduce himself. "Benjamin Mulcahey, Golden Age Task Force. It's a pleasure to meet you, Ma'am." He held out his hand and she shook it.

"Oh my, you sound like an Irishman," she observed. "Are you? I don't think I've ever met an Irishman before."

Ben blinked. "Yes, Ma'am. I'm originally from County Dublin."

Vera gasped "An honest-to-God Irishman in my house. I never thought I'd see the day." She turned to Rourke.

"Rourke Harken, Mrs. Berlin." Ben saw the edge of Rourke's smile twitch from the strain of being civil.

"No accent on you. Where are you from?" She asked.

Rourke shifted uncomfortably. "New Jersey."

"Oh, you have my condolences."

Arnold laughed and Rourke smiled nervously.

"Now, by all means, have a seat," Vera motioned to the couch. "Would you boys like some lemonade? I made it fresh this afternoon."

Arnold took a seat on the couch. "We would adore some, right fellas?"

"Yes, very much!" Ben took as a seat as well.

"Please," added Rourke, squeezing between Arnold and Ben.

Vera's lips stretched into what Ben assumed was a smile. He found it hard to look at. "It's the best you've ever tasted." She headed back into the kitchen.

When she was out of sight the three men stopped smiling. Rourke and Ben both found themselves rubbing their faces.

"So far, so good, boys," Arnold whispered. "We keep this up and we'll be fine."

Rourke shot him a look. "Am I the only one who is thoroughly freaked out?"

"Not any more than I was driving through the wasteland to get here," Ben reported. "I think I'm starting to get acclimated."

Arnold rolled his eyes at Rourke. "Get over how they look, will ya'? Vera's a good woman and the kids are terrific."

"Terrifying is more like it," Rourke whispered.

Ben elbowed his friend in the ribs, watching the stairs. "Cut it out."

Before any of them could press the issue further, Vera came back into the living room with a pitcher and three glasses of lemonade. With smiles firmly back in place, they all took a glass. It was sweet and so tart it made Ben's eyes water a little. He drank some more and decided that, yes. It was the best he had ever tasted.

"This is delicious, Mrs. Berlin," he said.

"Oh, do go on, Mister Mulcahey."

"What's all the commotion down there," a voice called out. They heard footsteps coming down the stairs.

He appeared in the living room seconds later. He wore a pair of gray wool trousers and a crisp white dress shirt with the collar opened. He was thin, muscular, his hair neatly buzzed and showing a hint of gray. He was clean-shaven, his Clubman aftershave filled the small living room. For a man bordering on ninety-five years old, he didn't look a day over forty-five.

He looked over the three men. His gaze hovering over each of them. Then, he smiled. It was a warm, friendly smile. "Arnold, you old so and so, how the heck are ya?"

Arnold stood up and wrung Troy's hand vigorously. "Ah, you know me, Troy. Wasting away in California." Troy laughed.

Rourke and Ben put down their glasses and stood up.

"Troy, these are the two guys I was tellin' you about over the phone. The fellas from the Task Force."

Troy nodded and his face changed from jovial to gravely serious.

"Agents, huh? Welcome to my home." He shook their hands. His grip was firm but not crushing. He was practiced and professional. "If there is anything I can do to assist in your investigation, I am at your service."

"Benjamin Mulcahey," Ben greeted. "This is my partner, Rourke Harken."

"Sir," Rourke nodded politely.

Troy nodded in return. "Of course, I'll need to see your credentials."

"Of course." Ben reached into his coat pocket and handed over his badge. Rourke did the same. Troy looked at each one carefully, then handed them back to the agents.

Troy turned to his wife, who was watching near the couch. He smiled at her.

"Vera, darling. When is dinner?"

"It should be ready in about twenty minutes."

"Would you be so kind as to go into the kitchen while the three of us talk over a few things? I'm afraid these men are here on business."

"Of course, Troy." She dutifully hurried back into the kitchen but not before giving her husband a peck on the cheek.

"She's great, isn't she?" Troy said.

Rourke smiled, "She makes one hell of a glass of lemonade."

Arnold winced. Troy's face twitched slightly.

"That she does, Agent Harken. But please, no cursing in my house, I have children."

Rourke blinked. "I am so sorry. I don't know what came over me."

Ben exhaled and was thankful Rourke's apology didn't have to come through a broken jaw.

Troy smiled warmly. "Think nothing of it. Sit."

"This is a lovely home you have here," Ben sipped his lemonade.

Troy turned a well-worn leather recliner to face the couch before taking a seat. "Thank you. Vera keeps a nice house." He paused. "So, Arnold told me you two are investigating the murder of Parker McCoy. You saw his body?"

Rourke replied. "That is correct."

Troy rubbed his chiseled jaw. "Incredible shame. He was a good man." He leaned in, "Deacon killed him, didn't he?"

Ben reached into his coat pocket and pulled out a small notepad and pen. "That's the prevailing theory."

Troy stared at Ben. "What are you doing?"

Ben's eyes widened. "Taking notes. For the investigation."

Troy's face twitched again. Ben's heart started to race.

"Ah, of course. How silly of me." Troy put them at ease.

"It is entirely possible he was killed by a copycat, but we discovered black mold around the bite wounds indicative of what was found on the bodies of previous victims."

Troy thought a moment. "I wouldn't call those people he ate victims, Agent Mulcahey. They were criminals, after all."

"Of course," Ben concurred. "Forensics is working on discerning if the mold is the same that was found on the perpetrators back in the Eighties."

"And if it's discovered that Deacon James killed Dr. McCoy, what then?" Troy asked. "Do you know how it is he was able to survive eight gunshots to the back?"

Rourke spoke up. "We were kinda' hoping maybe you'd be able to shed some light on that, Mister Berlin."

"Troy, please."

"You and Arnold were his closest friends. Did you know him to be bulletproof or have any sort of regenerative abilities?" Rourke queried.

"He never mentioned it. But then again, trying to get him to talk was like trying to get blood from a stone. Poor guy. I suppose it makes sense."

"What's that, Troy?" Arnold asked.

"That he'd survive getting shot. Only Rudy really knew the extent of his powers and by then, we'd all gone our separate ways." He leaned back in his chair. "But why would he want to kill Parker? What do you think, Arnold?"

"Honestly, I couldn't say. Kid was unstable to begin with, always had a faraway look in his eye. When he'd get itchy Parker would shoot him up with some kinda' serum and he'd be okay for a while. Maybe he got tired of being stuck like a lab experiment and just let whatever it was living inside him take over."

There was silence between them before Troy spoke again. "So, if your prevailing theory, agents, is that he's alive and killing again, what do you propose we do about it?"

Rourke answered. "Obviously we'd want to take him into custody if we can. When we discovered McCoy's body, the words 'find Howl' was written in McCoy's blood. We came to L.A. to warn Arnold. I suppose we're warning you, too."

Troy shook his head. "Deacon would never. We're friends."

"But wasn't he friends with Dr. McCoy?" Ben reminded.

"He's not himself. It's like Arnold said," Troy's voice was calm, but Ben sensed he could blow at any minute. "He wouldn't hurt me or my family." From the kitchen, Vera announced that dinner was ready.

Troy's face twitched again. "I hope you boys are hungry."

"Starved," Arnold lied.

"Good!" Troy stood up. "You'll find Vera's pot roast was well worth the trip."

•••

None of the china matched. As Ben sat down, he noticed fine cracks in his plate. It had been meticulously glued together at least once before. Bernadette and Maude both clamored for their father to pick them up and place them on their booster seats, squealing and giggling when he indulged them. It could've been a Rockwell painting, but for the broken plates, pulsing veins under translucent skin, and overblown plastic surgery. Ben had gone clammy watching Troy, The Automatic Man, relishing his role as father dearest. If Troy knew there was anything off or wrong about his household, he certainly wasn't showing it.

Ben felt a spike of guilt. If they were his kids or his wife, he probably wouldn't think anything of it.

"So," Troy clasped his hands together, "before we eat, who wants to say grace?"

Ben glanced over at Rourke. He expected an eye roll or a sigh, but thankfully, nothing of the sort occurred.

"Not me, old buddy," Arnold begged off. "I ain't Catholic."

"Ain't isn't a word, is it Maude?" Troy looked at his half-albino daughter. She giggled happily.

"That's right Daddy. You'd say "I'm not Catholic," Uncle Arnold."

Arnold chuckled.

Ben slowly raised his hand. "Mr. Berlin, I'm Catholic. I'd be happy to." He lied about his religion to keep things calm and pleasant. He felt icy fingers wrapping around his spine. He hadn't bothered saying grace in years, but Ben was genuinely afraid of Troy Berlin. At this point, he was just trying to get out alive.

"That would be fine." Troy motioned for his family to bow their heads, as he bowed his. Troy made the sign of the cross and his family followed.

Arnold and Rourke did not. Rourke didn't even put his head down. Ben's forehead beaded up with sweat. He was silent for a moment, trying to remember the old Catholic dinner prayer.

"Bless us, oh Lord, for these, thy gifts which we are about to receive from thy bounty through Christ our Lord, Amen." He crossed himself as did Troy and his family.

Suddenly Bernadette giggled.

"You talk funny," she grinned. It showed more of her baby teeth and a few adult molars.

Ben's face flushed.

"Bernadette!" Vera chided.

Troy looked down his nose at Bernadette sternly.

"Uh oh!" Maude said. "You're in trouble!"

"I talk funny?" Ben asked.

Bernadette shook her head, it made the bulging vein near her temple throb faster.

"That's because I come from another country," he explained.

"Agent Mulcahey is from Ireland. Girls, what is the capital city of Ireland?" Troy quizzed.

The girls said in their eerie harmony, "Dublin in the south, Glasgow in the north."

Ben smiled, despite the goosebumps rising on his skin. "That's very good."

"We homeschool our children, Mr. Mulcahey," Vera said proudly. "This way they actually learn something." Troy handed her his plate. She put a helping of carrots, an unidentifiable piece of meat, and mashed potatoes on it and passed it back to him.

"Too much liberal propaganda in the classroom these days," Troy declared. "Last thing I want is for my daughters to be brainwashed."

Ben nodded solemnly. This family was definitely a living testament to the dangers of brainwashing.

Vera took Ben's plate and dish, her smile never fading or wavering. He had to admit it, the carrots and potatoes looked great. As she handed back his plate, he eyed the mystery meat. He was guessing it was some sort of pot roast with rich brown gravy. The smell was working its way into his nose, making his mouth water. The roasted carrots smelled like they were glazed with honey and the mashed potatoes swam in butter. It was definitely was the kind of Americana that Americans didn't even believe in anymore.

She served the others and they commenced eating. Troy had to cut Maude and Bernadette's dinners into small pieces. Neither of them used a fork. Only spoons.

"I tell you," Troy continued, "this whole situation wouldn't have happened if people didn't vote for those brain-dead liberals."

Ben shot a glance over at Rourke, but Rourke must have pretended not to have heard. He was focused on cutting his pot roast.

"What do you mean, Troy?" Arnold shoveled a forkful of potatoes into his mouth.

"I mean had we been able to do our jobs all these years, things would be different," Troy argued. "Take those two buildings in New York for instance."

Rourke looked up from his plate and over to Troy. "You mean the Trade Center?"

"Yes, Agent Harken, I do." He pointed his fork at Rourke. "Had the Exceptional People's Act still been in effect, those lousy camel jockeys wouldn't have gotten near those buildings."

The girls giggled at the term "camel jockey".

Vera shushed them. "Girls, your father is talking."

The girls stopped.

Ben watched Rourke's movements slow, his chewing strained and deliberate. Ben could tell Rourke desperately wanted to argue with Troy. It took every ounce of strength he had not to.

"Aw, come on, Troy. We're old shoe," Arnold suggested. "The world moved on from superheroes."

"Yeah, and now Parker McCoy is dea..." He stopped himself. "Now Parker is gone. We could have stopped Deacon. Gotten him better help."

"That we could have. That is if it was Deacon who done it."

"Did it," Maude echoed.

Arnold smiled at her.

"I've been thinking about that," Troy said through a mouthful of carrots. "It wasn't a copy-cat."

"What makes you so sure?" Rourke took a sip of water.

"Because of what Agent Mulcahey said earlier about the mold around the wound. There is no way that could be replicated and I'm sure the tests will come back confirming it." Troy looked at Ben as if to see if Ben would corroborate his theory.

Ben leaned back in his chair. "I'd be inclined to agree with you, Mister Berlin, but for the sake of the investigation we can't rule anything out."

Troy's face twitched slightly. "Of course, Agent."

Ben swallowed a lump in his throat.

Rourke rubbed his forehead. "Did McCoy have any enemies?"

"No," Arnold replied. "Parker was a lot of things, but he never went out of his way to make enemies."

"So he never fought supervillains directly?"

"He was really just the architect of the Golden Age," Troy recalled. "You never met a more upstanding guy. Granted, back in the old days some of the more powerful guys wanted a crack at him but they never got close enough."

"Hm." Rourke hummed. He took a bite of meat. "This is delicious, Mrs. Berlin." He actually meant it.

Vera smiled warmly.

"Daddy?" Bernadette said. "What happened to Uncle Parker?"

"Uncle Deacon did something bad," Maude said.

Troy looked at them both again with a stern, fatherly look. "Girls, adults are talking. When adults are talking children should be seen and not heard."

The girls frowned and said in unison, "Yes, daddy."

Troy's face flushed. "You'll have to excuse my daughters, Agents. They are quite perceptive."

"Quite all right, Mister Berlin. Perhaps we should speak after dinner?" Ben suggested.

"Yes, Agent Mulcahey. I think that would be a good idea."

They ate in silence for the remainder of the meal. Vera and the girls quietly left the dinner table and let Troy and his guests resume their conversation.

"My girls," Troy started, "have a very rosy view of Parker McCoy and I like to keep it that way." He picked at a carrot left on his plate. "We haven't told them what happened just yet."

"It seems Maude already knows," Arnold pointed out.

"Like I said, she's perceptive."

"Maybe she's got that ESP stuff," Arnold offered.

"What sort of heathen suggestion is that," Troy retorted through clenched teeth. "My children are just incredibly bright, that's all."

Arnold waved his hand. "You're probably right."

Troy cleared his throat. "As I was saying, we like to keep a rosy picture of Parker in our house, for the girls' sake, but to truly answer your question, Agent Harken, Parker McCoy had many enemies."

"How many of them wanted him dead?" Rourke queried.

"Depends. How many stars are in the sky?"

Arnold let out a small laugh. "Look, we put on a good show for the girls, but you don't get to be the guy engineering Golden Age policy without putting a target on your back."

"Could it be possible that, if Deacon is indeed alive and it's not a copycat, that one of McCoy's enemies could have gotten to Deacon?" Ben asked.

Arnold pulled his chin. "You mean like, convinced Deacon to kill Parker?"

"Precisely. Or, would Deacon have a reason to kill McCoy?"

"Right," Rourke said. "Would there have been a reason for the two of them to be at odds?"

Troy and Arnold looked at each other. "No," Arnold answered. "Deacon needed Parker. For the injections."

"That's right," Troy confirmed. "They stopped him from getting itchy and eating people. Though, I wouldn't have given him so much."

Rourke raised his eyebrow. "What do you mean?"

"I mean, the guys he ate were scum and deserved to die. That plain enough for you, Agent Harken?"

"Easy, Troy," Arnold cautioned. "I don't think Deacon would have killed McCoy unless he was conned into doing it. He was a weird guy, like I've said about a hundred times, but he'd never hurt one of us. We were his friends."

Ben scratched his head. "Right, but how close was he to Doctor McCoy? Putting aside your feelings for him, Arnold."

Arnold mulled it over. "Puttin' it that way, Irish, I suppose they wasn't so close. That don't mean..."

"No," Ben interrupted. "It doesn't establish any sort of motive, but it's possible that there could be something there. A resentment maybe. Troy, how well did you know Deacon prior to him eating people?"

"Deacon was a hard man to know," Troy admitted. "Rudy was the one he confided in, I think."

"Yeah, in our file on him, redacted all to hell as it was, it mentioned that he didn't speak much," Rourke informed them. "It must have been hard as hell for you guys to figure out what was going on with him."

If Troy was offended by the word 'hell' he didn't show it, not even a facial twitch. "Yes. It made being his teammate very difficult, but it was different back then. We just accepted it as part of his...exceptionality, let's call it."

"Rudyard Sinclair, The Swami, he spoke to Deacon fairly regularly? You know this for a fact?" Ben took out his notebook and pen from his jacket pocket.

Arnold shrugged again, "I guess so. I think that medallion had a lot to do with it."

Rourke looked over at Arnold. "You're talking about what Rudy referred to as the Medallion of Delphi, right?"

"That heathen thing he wore around his neck," Troy remembered. "I refuse to believe in any of that satanic hocus pocus."

Rourke dismissed this. "You think it let Rudyard in somehow? Let him know what was going on in Deacon's head?"

"I suppose it's possible. I never really asked him. That thing always gave me the jeebies," Arnold confessed. "Despite what Troy here thinks, that medallion did some strange stuff."

"Parker always wanted to test that thing but Rudy wouldn't let him," Troy added. "If Deacon trusted anyone, it was definitely Rudy."

Ben asked, "Why was that, do you figure?"

"I couldn't say. They had a connection, I guess. It started after the incident with the senator's daughter."

Rourke looked at Ben, who was scribbling notes. "They confided in each other?"

"Maybe. Pretty soon after that, things got bad and everyone hung up their capes. We went home," Troy's words had a bitter edge.

Ben sighed. "The biggest problem we're facing, Mister Berlin, is the fact that Deacon or someone like him is out there and he's looking for Arnold. I don't presume to know why he'd want to kill him, aside from what we already know about his unstable...er...eating habits."

Rourke added, "At this point, it's safe to assume that if it is Deacon that killed Parker, he's so far gone he can't differentiate between friend or foe. What's more is, should we apprehend him somewhere along the line, we don't exactly know how to hold Deacon or how to kill him. We know bullets won't work."

"Do either of you even have any idea," Troy asked, "where Deacon is currently?"

Rourke stared at Troy blankly.

"We hadn't stopped to consider where else Deacon may have been headed," Ben admitted. "We acted on the assumption that he was heading to California to finish off the Crimson Howl."

"But if that's the case, why did Deacon write who he was trying to find on the wall unless he wanted to be apprehended?" Troy puzzled.

"We've been in the dark as to his motivation," Rourke sighed. "We assumed he was going to Los Angeles. Arnold's house is basically public knowledge. It made sense that's where he would head."

"But you managed to get there before Deacon did. Then, you used Arnold to find me."

"Obviously," Arnold nodded. "Where you goin' with this, Troy?"

"Maybe, and this is just a hunch so bear with me, gentlemen. Maybe Deacon was forced to kill McCoy and knowing someone would see the gory writing on the wall, wrote about finding The Crimson Howl not because he was going to be his next victim, but because he needed his help."

It dawned on Ben that they had gotten rusty. Being reduced to little more than glorified paper pushers, they'd taken too much for granted.

"The thought had crossed my mind, but it didn't make sense to me. He was presumed dead in a hail of gunfire, only to reappear after having had his fill of a Golden Age VIP. That seems more about vengeance than about an SOS signal."

"The message could easily be a simple cry for help. He'd done it in the past. It's the reason we took him to McCoy in the first place," Troy defended his idea. "If we run with this theory, gentlemen, we'd still have to establish two things, who could get close enough to Deacon to convince him to kill McCoy and why would that person want to have him killed?"

Arnold's face turned grim. "You ain't supposin'..."

Troy returned Arnold's look with a serious one of his own. "It's a long shot, but he's our best option."

Ben and Rourke both looked equally puzzled. "Who are you talking about?"

Troy gave them a half smile. "Isn't it obvious, Agents?"

Arnold looked at them. "He's talking about Rudyard Sinclair. If you want in Deacon's head, he's your man."

"You mentioned Sinclair earlier," Rourke said. "Do you think he influenced Deacon somehow and turned him on Parker?"

"It's possible I suppose. Rudy never struck me as the type to use someone else to lash out. I always got the impression he'd torment them himself if he was so inclined," Troy said. "Besides, why would Rudy want McCoy dead? Even when the doc wanted to study his infernal medallion, he was more amused than anything."

"We keep talking about his accomplishments, but can anyone answer me one question? What kind of man was McCoy?" Rourke wanted to know.

Troy leaned forward. "I met him first out of any of us. He was the man who made me what I am today. I don't remember a lot about the early days though. There are pieces missing when I try to remember exactly what it was like when they were making me."

"Don't worry. As usual, I have your back Troy," Arnold affirmed. "Troy might not remember, but McCoy told me the story a half dozen times of how Troy was the only one to survive the experiments. Maybe there's something there you can use. It was back in '38..."

CHAPTER FOURTEEN

June 1938
A Military Installation in New Mexico

"That you, Doc?"

"Yes, Troy, it's me. May I come in?"

"Of course, Doc. No need to be so darned polite!" Troy called from where he was sat at the wooden table, his food tray empty. Troy had a pack of Chesterfields on the table. McCoy saw he had smoked three of them and was nearly finished with a fourth. McCoy didn't like his subjects smoking.

"How are you feeling today?" He took Troy's wrist and checked his pulse. It was normal.

"Pretty good, Doc. Good eats tonight. Meatloaf. Better than my ma's. That ain't sayin' a whole lot. Ma don't cook so good." He smiled and stubbed his smoke out in the metal tray.

Troy was, for all intents and purposes, a normal, healthy nineteen-year-old. He was by no means skinny like so many of the others who had signed up for these tests because of the promise of three meals a day; his muscles were still developing and would continue to do so as the experiments went on. He wore the standard issue OD olive green pants the Army quartermaster had given him an Army issue buzzcut. His dogtags hung loosely over his athletic shirt. A record player, the volume set very low, churned out a Benny Goodman tune.

"I'm glad you're enjoying the food. The room is still to your liking?"

"It's swell Doc. I only wish I had a window. That picture ain't really cuttin' it." He gestured behind him to a picture, cut from a copy of LIFE Magazine of a sandy beach in Hawaii. "Not that I'm complaining, I sure am grateful for everything. My ma is too. She thinks the world of you and that's sayin' somethin'. She don't usually like nig..." Troy's face turned red. "I mean, colored guys."

McCoy laughed. "I'm glad I'm the exception. She got the check, I suppose?"

"Oh, sure. It's been a big help, the extra dough. Since Pop died workin' on the railroad, it's been hard for her."

McCoy nodded.

"I'm more than happy to help your family in any way I can, son." It was hard for McCoy to sound like he cared for the boy, as despite his fondness for him, Troy was little more than a lab rat in a very lethal test.

"So, how am I doin', Doc? I tell yah, I feel terrific. Like I can do just about anything!"

"I'm more than happy to help your family…"

"Well, so far you've passed all of my tests with flying colors. Your strength and endurance have exceeded measurable levels in a human being. Pretty soon we'll be able to move on to phase two. That is if we can find the funding."

Troy's expression saddened. "I guess your big meeting didn't go so good, huh?"

"I'm afraid not. But the good news is the President himself assured me he would find the money somehow."

Troy spat. "That goddamn Roosevelt. All he does is spend money and all we get is alphabet soup!"

This made McCoy laugh. "Easy, son. Don't forget, as a soldier in the Army, he's your boss."

Troy picked up his pack of Chesterfields and shook one out. "Smoke, Doc?"

McCoy waved his hand dismissively. "No, thank you."

Troy lit his cigarette before asking, "So what's phase two? Or am I not allowed to know that yet?" There was no hint of condescension in his voice, no fear either. He was genuinely eager to move on. McCoy liked that.

"Normally, I would have to tell you it's classified, but I don't think it matters at this point. Tell me, Troy, would you mind if we subjected you to a minor surgery?"

"Surgery? Like before with the injections after you took my blood?"

"I'm afraid it's a bit more invasive. I'd need to have a look at that brain of yours." McCoy tensed as he saw Troy turn white.

"Whoa, Doc. My brain? That don't sound like no minor surgery to me." He took a long drag on his cigarette. "What do you aim to do to my brain anyhow?"

"Troy, I've made you stronger, faster, and have given you reflexes far beyond those of regular men. Those things are all fine and good, but for what I need, what your country needs, is a man who knows how to fight. What I need to do is get into your brain and make a few adjustments."

"You mean like tuning a radio?"

McCoy had to admit the boy caught on quick. "Yes. Just like that. If you ever go into combat and you get caught, we need to make sure you won't give away state secrets. Not that it's a concern of mine. Though you aren't bulletproof, you're so fast a bullet would never hit you. Those reflexes of yours will be... what's the word... automatic. See, I can program you; I can implant certain things, suggestions if you will, which will allow you to learn things in a matter of minutes. That too, will be automatic. You'll be a regular automatic man."

"I think you lost me, Doc."

"Name something you've always wanted to do but was too hard for you?"

Troy thought a moment. "I always wanted to play the piano. My ma said I don't have the fingers for it."

"Well, after this surgery you'd be able to pick up the piano in a matter of days. Hell, you could be a regular Mozart if you wanted to. All I have to do is make a few adjustments. A fine-tuning, if you will."

Troy's eyes widened. "No foolin'?"

"No foolin'. But Troy, here's the rub. It's going to be a few years before you're going to see any sort of combat."

"I know, Doc."

"And while the prospect of you languishing here with me in a lab in New Mexico must sound terrible to you…"

Troy cut in. "You ain't been nothing but good to me and my ma, Doc."

"Let me finish, son! Things are in the works right now where we may be able to put your new skills to good use."

"Really?"

"Let me tell you a bit about The Exceptional Peoples Act."

•••

Troy interrupted Arnold. "I can take over from here. This much I remember."

•••

The nurse knocked on the door at six in the morning and entered after Troy told her he was decent. Troy had been up since four, too nervous to sleep. The Doc had said no food so Troy spent half the night smoking and listening to his jazz records.

"Doctor McCoy is ready for you now, Mister Berlin," the nurse reported.

"Thanks." Maybe later, once all this was over with he'd show her a thing or two.

She led him to a gurney and instructed him to lie down on it.

Troy got on the gurney. He squinted. He never noticed how ugly the overhead lights were in this corridor, nor how quiet it had gotten over the past few months. The nurse unlocked the gurney's wheels and slowly walked the stretcher down the hallway. Troy tried to flirt with the nurse a little but she was a real cold fish. All business. Troy hadn't had much luck with girls despite his boyish good looks and muscular physique. He never seemed to be able to think of anything to say to them.

Maybe after the surgery he'd have better luck. Doc said he'd be able to pick up things quicker than most guys.

The gurney stopped at a set of large double doors. The doors had no windows like the others in the hallway. The nurse knocked three times and waited for it to open.

"Doctors. They always make you wait," Troy joked. She looked at him but didn't smile. "You know, you'd be a lot more attractive if you smiled every now and then. You'll never get a husband with a frown like the one you got."

Before the nurse had a chance to reply, the right-side door opened. Doctor McCoy stood in the doorway. He was wearing a blue-collar shirt and gray slacks.

"Thank you, Vera. That will be all." The nurse turned and walked away, not giving Troy even so much as a glance.

"Some dame," Troy grumbled. "Where'd you find her?"

Before he answered, McCoy came around and pushed the gurney into the room. "Vera is my best staff nurse. Doesn't take shit from anyone. Not even me."

McCoy wheeled Troy through another set of double doors and into the operating room. It was small, almost cramped. Big machines covered the walls, blinking lights flashed on and off, and gave out a small humming drone. There was a small tray with gleaming steel instruments, sharp and deadly if used improperly; precise and healing if used the way they were intended. The gurney stopped over a bright overhead lamp. Troy blinked into the light, trying to focus.

"I have to introduce you to the man who is going to be operating today." McCoy was looking down at Troy when he spoke but looked up when he said, "You can come in now, Doctor."

A voice from above Troy spoke. "Good morning, Mr. Berlin." He finally came into Troy's view. He was an older guy, way older than the Doc. He was wearing thick, black-rimmed glasses, his hair graying curls. There were a couple of liver spots in his cheeks and forehead. He was wearing what appeared to be an apron. "I'm Doctor Joe Newglory." He didn't try to shake Troy's hand.

"Yeah. Great name." Troy lifted his head up to look at McCoy. "This guy is gonna go into my brain? Not for nothin', Doc but this guy's a thousand!"

McCoy smiled. "You have nothing to worry about, Troy."

"Mr. Berlin, I'm only sixty-one," Dr. Newglory said. "I've been doing brain operations since before you were in diapers."

"I've known Dr. Newglory for a long time, son," McCoy added. "I hand-picked him specifically for this operation. He's been on stand-by for the duration of the project just waiting for his skills to be called into use."

Troy relaxed on the gurney. His heart beat slower now as a certain relief spread over him. If the Doc said he was ok, then he was ok. He was just peachy.

McCoy looked over Troy, "You can still back out. No shame in getting cold feet."

For a split second, Troy almost did. Then he thought about The Crimson Howl; about the man waging war against the mobs and liberals and filth out there on the streets. That could still be him, Troy Berlin, out there fighting. He could be a hero. He could be The Automatic Man, and usher in what Doctor McCoy had called the Golden Age. In his lifetime, they could see such a decrease in crime in the country that decent people could walk through the worst neighborhoods without fear.

"Nah, Doc. Let's get started."

McCoy nodded to his colleague. "You heard the man, Joe. Let's get started."

"Wait!" Troy raised a hand. "I gotta ask you. What happens if I don't make it? Does my ma get cut off?"

McCoy understood Troy's concerns. "No, Troy. The checks will keep coming."

"Ok, Doc, then let's go." The next thing he knew, Dr. Newglory put his surgical mask on and placed a black rubber face mask on Troy. He told him to breathe deeply and count backwards from ten. As he counted down his vision got black around the edges, before he kicked off to a deep, dreamless sleep, the dead eye of the hanging light came on. Troy swore he saw it wink at him before the room and his entire world went black.

•••

Doctor McCoy entered the room with Doctor Newglory and the blonde nurse, Vera. Everyone except for Vera was smiling.

"Good afternoon Troy!" McCoy greeted. "Glad to see you've finally woken up. How do you feel, son?"

"Like I got hit by the same train that killed my old man." His voice was low, a whisper, as if speaking any louder would shatter his brain. "I guess I did okay, seeing as how I ain't dead."

"You did fine. Just fine." He reached into his pocket and pulled out a fresh pack of Chesterfields. "Smoke, Troy?"

Troy looked at the pack of cigarettes as if he'd never seen them before. "I don't smoke, Doc. You know that."

A smile of satisfaction spread across McCoy's face.

Dr. Newglory said, "The operation was successful, however there was a very minor complication."

McCoy stopped smiling.

"Complication?" Troy asked. "What do you mean?"

Dr. Newglory cleared his throat. "Well, you have to understand you've been unconscious for two weeks. In that time Dr. McCoy and I have been altering certain parts of your brain. A week ago, as we were implanting certain commands you..."

"Troy," McCoy pointed at Newglory. "Kill him!"

Before the old surgeon could protest Troy was out of bed. His hands shot out as fists, smashing into the elderly doctor. Troy's strikes connected with a vicious precision, bones crunching under them. By the time he fell, Dr. Newglory was already dead of a cracked windpipe, a ruptured spleen, and about sixteen broken ribs, one of which had splintered and pierced the old surgeon's heart. It wasn't until Troy fell back onto the bed that he realized what happened.

McCoy's eyes shined. Vera stood emotionless.

"Very good, Troy," he applauded.

Suddenly a look of bewilderment came over Troy. "Doc? What happened? Oh shit!" he looked down at the dead Doctor Newglory. "What happened to him?"

"You killed him, Troy. Had to be done. I discovered today the man was a Nazi sympathizer. Bastard. I trusted him. You saved our lives, Troy."

Troy still looked puzzled, "I...I did?"

"Yes, son. Vera, get one of the orderlies to come clean this up. Troy and I have a lot of catching up to do."

"Right away, Doctor." Vera exited the room in no real hurry. Troy's head started to feel better and he no longer felt sick.

"You like her?" McCoy inquired already knowing the answer.

"She's a real dish, Doc, but I think she's out of my league."

"I don't think so. In fact, I have a feeling the two of you will hit it off the next couple of weeks while your body adjusts to that new brain of yours."

"If you say so, Doc." The pain in Troy's head was almost gone now. "The Doctor said something about a complication. What did he mean by that?"

"Newglory messed up," McCoy explained. "He made an incision too long in your frontal lobe which means that every now and again, for no reason whatsoever, your brain is gonna go haywire." He hesitated before adding, "I think the bastard may have done it sabotage us. Damned Nazis."

Troy looked perplexed. "What do you mean, haywire?"

"In terms you'd understand, Troy, it's like static on a radio. Information is coming at you every second of every day and when this information gets jumbled in your brain, you'll sort of zone out a bit. You'll do things, more than likely things you would never do while conscious. I've implanted a lot of things in your head, Troy. You can fight better than anyone, and you'll never give away state secrets but if you aren't careful, if you are under a great deal of stress or get angry for whatever reason, your mind is going to go haywire and you'll go blank and the next thing you know, something beyond your control will have happened."

Troy thought about it for a moment. "Is this going to be a problem?"

"No. You'll just have to learn to control it."

"Can't you just go back in there and fix what's wrong?"

"No. Even if I wanted to it's too damned risky. We'd wind up killing you and I can't allow that."

"I understand," Troy didn't want to sound disappointed but he couldn't help it. Suddenly, he wondered if this meant his career as a crime fighter would be over before it started. "How will this affect your plans for me?"

McCoy rubbed his chin, which had gone a few days without a proper shave. "I don't think we'll concern ourselves with that right now. We've gotta get that little problem of yours under control before we let you out into the world."

"I understand. Sorry I let you down, Doc."

McCoy chuckled. "You had nothing to do with it, Troy. That traitor Newglory was to blame and you took care of him." McCoy stood up. "Rest assured, The Automatic Man will have his day in the sun. I promise you that."

•••

In the fall of 1938, a creature out of a nightmare assaulted New York City. It was impossibly tall and bony, a narrow face and receding hairline. Even in a city like New York where people were hardened to the day-to-day violence of metropolitan living, people were fleeing in terror. There had been urban legends of fiendish gas attacks since The Great War and this gaunt figure was fear made flesh. Supposed scores were dead as the fiend unleashed mustard gas clouds from the canister strapped to his back.

Then in the first week of November 1938. Troy Berlin, the Automatic Man, and the Crimson Howl showed up during one of The Doctor's gas raids and proceeded to pummel the man into submission. Of course, miraculously, The Doctor got away, vowing he'd return and finish The Automatic Man and The Crimson Howl once and for all. No one was seriously hurt and the new masked vigilante was hailed a hero (but misnamed in the media. An eye witness had said he was so fast it was like watching a human bullet and the name sort of stuck, much to Troy's chagrin.) New York was safe once more. It was the beginning of The Golden Age.

Troy loved every second of it. He'd patrol the streets alone mostly. It wouldn't be until 1939 that he and the Crimson Howl became officially sanctioned partners in crime-fighting, and he was glad to see the Doc's plan come to fruition. Every other day it seemed a new costumed do-gooder was out fighting. He had read stories in foreign newspapers that the phenomenon wasn't just confined to American shores. Costumed heroes were popping up in Europe and even in Hong Kong and India. The Exceptional People's Act was passed unanimously and those young men who were able, who had a sense of right and wrong, and who could sew a costume were deputized by local police commissioners and given a modest paycheck every month.

Of course, most of these men were just regular guys with no powers of their own. As far as he knew, Troy was the only guy with any sort of special abilities. The Crimson Howl had razor blades sewn into his gloves and had the speed and strength of a prizefighter. He could take and receive a good beating and smile at either one. Troy admired his courage. He'd have to talk to McCoy and see what he could do to help his new colleague.

The legitimate phenoms, the real Exceptionals started popping up in 1939 as well. It was said at the time that McCoy had a hand in every last one of them. The Mermaid was a pet project of his, combining amphibian DNA with a human. Mr. Indestructible was another, a bulletproof brute of a man. Each one of them would leave their mark on their respective city and each one would eventually be forced to retire when Nixon took office and McCoy fell out of favor with the government. Too much money was being spent turning regular people into Exceptionals and their popularity was fading. Vietnam had made Americans skeptical of government "heroes," military or otherwise.

Without voter backing, the politicians pulled the plug on the whole operation. The superheroes, no longer on the government dole, but given a pension for the work they had done, hung up their capes and went back to their mundane lives. As the heroes disappeared, so did the supervillains and their grandiose plans. Most of them were already in prison and once the Act was repealed, they were paroled and told to go home and stay out of trouble. Most, surprisingly, did.

The day the Act was repealed was a sad day for Troy Berlin. Despite being one of the heroes who had successfully served his country in World War Two and pummeled the likes of The Aryan in Germany, who saved a little girl with the help of his best friends from a satanic child rapist, he simply came home to his wife Vera one hot day in May and hung up his cape and tights in his bedroom closet.

He stood there for a good long while. His tights had been torn in nearly a dozen places over the years, and Vera had always patched them up for him whenever they needed mending. His cape fluttered in the wind like Old Glory on a battleship. The way it broadened his shoulders, the way it made him feel stronger than he was, hung limp in the closet.

"They don't need us anymore," he said quietly. Vera was standing behind him looking as young as the day they met. He'd never let her see it, but a tear rolled down his cheek as he closed the closet door.

He rubbed his eye and turned to face his wife.

"I guess I'll just have to be Troy Berlin: Family Man instead of The Automatic Man, huh?"

Vera often worried about her husband, the man she was in love with but didn't really know why. They had two children together. Two beautiful girls. She had read terrible things in the papers about Troy and his temper but she didn't believe a word of it. He was nothing but sweet and gentle around her and the girls. Having him home for good would be the best thing for him. For all of them.

"That sounds good to me, Troy, darling." She said, her voice was like tinkling bells, just a hint of a southern drawl.

CHAPTER FIFTEEN

Rourke awoke with a start. The fact that Troy's daughter Maude was a few inches from his face didn't help at all.

"Daddy says it's time for you to get up," she said, smiling wide. She held a steaming mug of coffee. "Here!"

"Wha...?"

Now he remembered. It had gotten too late for them to leave and Troy suggested they spend the night and start fresh in the morning. Rourke had taken the couch and Ben curled up on a beat-up La-Z-Boy. Arnold claimed the guest bedroom. "What time is it?" he asked. Maude simply shrugged.

"Time to get a watch," she said and giggled.

Rourke took the mug of coffee from her.

"Yeah, I guess it is. Thanks." Though the girls were hard to look at, he had to admit they sorta grew on him a little. They were creepy but spunky.

He looked over and saw Bernadette standing over Ben. She was also holding a cup of coffee, waiting for Ben to wake up.

"Why don't you let me give that to him," Rourke whispered. "Give him some time to sleep a little more, huh?"

Bernadette frowned a little but did as she was asked. She handed Rourke the coffee and the two girls scampered off. He took a sip of his coffee. It was very strong, like the Turkish coffee Jill had been fond of. It was also cloyingly sweet. He guessed the girls had their hands in that. He took a gulp of coffee and it burned all the way down. Rourke shivered and he set the cup down. Then, stood up and went over to Ben.

"Get up," he shook his partner a little.

Ben awoke. and he too looked slightly out of sorts. "Where? Oh right. We spent the night."

"Here. Drink this," Rourke held out the mug of coffee to Ben, careful not to spill it. Ben took a sip. He grimaced.

"Bejesus, that's terrible." He took another sip.

"Just down it and be thankful it's me handing it to you. You almost woke up to Bernadette a couple inches from your face."

"Good lord, I think you've saved me from a heart attack," Ben sniffed at his armpit. "Do you think Troy will let me take a shower? I'm a little ripe."

Before Rourke had time to answer Troy descended the steps in what could only be called an excited traipse. He was wearing suit pants, a white button-down shirt, and a black tie. He was clean-shaven and neatly groomed. Once more the smell of aftershave preceded him.

"Good morning, agents," he greeted. "We haven't much time. When Arnold is out of the shower and dressed we are leaving immediately."

"Well, there goes your shower," Rourke said. Ben frowned.

"Apologies, agents. We have no time to lose. Did you have coffee?"

Both men nodded.

"Good. The girls make it a little strong for my taste, but I don't need caffeine." The three men stood in silence while they waited for Arnold. Rourke wasn't sure about Ben but he didn't feel like risking small talk. Arnold's heavy footsteps on the staircase were a relief.

"Troy, I ain't your bellboy. Take this suitcase." Arnold was lugging what appeared to be a valise from the fifties.

"Sorry, old friend. I know how heavy it must be for you." Troy met Arnold halfway up the stairs and grabbed the suitcase.

"Wait a second," Rourke said. "What's with the suitcase?"

Troy looked at Rourke. "Isn't it obvious?"

"No. Are you... going somewhere?"

Troy looked at Arnold and shared a laugh. "I'm coming with you. I can help you both with your investigation."

Rourke sighed. This was starting to get ridiculous. So far, they'd traveled all the way out to California to warn one of their VIPs that his life was in danger and that snowballed into driving deep into New Mexico to find a family of extras from The Hills Have Eyes. Now their working theory was that a mystical fruitcake might have convinced a super-powered cannibal to kill the guy who set off this madness back during the Depression.

"Mister Berlin, don't you think you'd be better off staying here with your family? We're more than capable of handling this investigation."

A twitch under Troy's right eye suggested that, no, he would not be better off staying here with his family.

"Rourke, let's not be too hasty. Perhaps Mister Berlin can help us," Ben interjected. "We don't have any idea where Rudyard lives. And much like having Arnold with us, having Troy along might be beneficial. Rudyard might not talk to us." He winked at Rourke.

Troy looked at Arnold.

"I told yah," Arnold grinned. "The Irish kid is good. The pipsqueak's got a mouth on 'im."

Troy nodded. "I appreciate your concern, Agent Harken but I'm fully capable of taking care of myself. Besides, Parker McCoy was my friend and if Rudyard had anything to do with his death, I want to know why. Agent Mulcahey does touch upon some very valid points. I do know where Rudyard lives and I know for a fact that he won't talk to either of you. He's distrustful by nature. Years of living in the closet and all."

Rourke heaved an exasperated sigh, "Alright. Where are we going?"

"A place I would imagine is familiar to the both of you." Troy pulled what appeared to be a postcard from his trouser pocket and handed it to Rourke.

The card showed a beach and an old wooden boardwalk with a Ferris wheel and a roller coaster. Chunky block lettering bespeckled with multicolored dots announced cheerfully "GREETINGS FROM SEASIDE HEIGHTS".

Rourke couldn't help but chuckle. He and Ben had spent a great deal of time down there as teenagers. Going down the shore in the summer was a New Jersey tradition like pork roll or great pizza. He gave Ben the postcard.

"Of course we know it. Spent a lot of time down there. Wasted a lot of my allowance on those stupid boardwalk games. Won a goldfish once. It died before we got home." Rourke paused. "Of all the places for Rudyard to be holed up, why there?"

Troy held his hands palms up. "Beats me. New Jersey isn't exactly…nice."

"That's not true," Ben disagreed. "There's lots of nice places."

Arnold snorted. "The nicest smelling turd in the bowl is still a turd, Irish."

This got the two former superheroes laughing. Rourke had to admit it was pretty funny.

"Troy! Troy don't forget your garment bag!" Vera hurried down the stairs carrying a thin garment bag. Two hangar heads were visible. Vera herself was a sight to behold, her face plastered in cold cream.

Rourke's eyes darted to the floor so he wouldn't have to look at her.

Troy took the bag. "I'd forget my head if it weren't attached. Thank you, dear." She hurried back up the stairs for which Rourke was grateful.

"Well, I suggest we get going. We've got a long trip ahead of us," Troy stated the obvious.

The two men walked towards the front door. Rourke stopped them.

"You mean we're driving all the way to New Jersey? At this point, it would be easier to fly, right?" He looked to Ben, "Right?"

Troy gave him a condescending smile. "My boy, do you really want me going haywire at thirty-seven thousand feet? I'd kill us all."

Troy opened the door and was about to exit when Maude and Bernadette called after him.

"Oh!" Troy turned around to face his children. "You didn't think I would forget to say goodbye, did you?"

The girls giggled. "Nuh-uh," they said in harmony.

Maude stretched her arms out and Troy hugged her first. "You'll be back, right Daddy?"

Troy kissed his half-albino daughter on the palest part of her cheek. "Of course!"

Bernadette joined her sister in the embrace. Troy looked at both girls. "Now, who can stop The Automatic Man?" he asked in a booming voice.

"No one," Maude said with glee.

"Except Mama," Bernadette added and the three had a good laugh.

Rourke thought it would be touching if the girls weren't so damned creepy and Troy wasn't a certifiable lunatic.

"Come on, Troy," Arnold called. "We're burning daylight."

"Be good now, mind your mama." Troy gave his daughters one final hug and kiss and the men exited Troy's home into the cool predawn morning.

Ben helped Troy with his bags and Arnold got into the passenger seat. Ben gave Troy the keys as Troy climbed into the driver's seat. Rourke waved Ben over.

In a hushed voice, he said, "This doesn't smell right."

"I know."

"If you know, then why is that lunatic, psychopath, crazy man coming with us?"

"Because we need him, Rourke. Look, just trust me on this. I have a plan. If you think these guys are in control, you're nuts. The easiest and best way for us to find Deacon and bring him in is to let these three bloodhounds find him. Follow?"

Rourke raised an eyebrow. "So, the hero worship is just an act? Please tell me it's just an act."

"I'm not going to lie and say it is. Just believe me that it isn't all just hero worship."

"Shit," Rourke cursed. The sun was starting to rise across the desert. "Well, we'd better get going. Lay you ten to one odds he goes nuts because someone cut him off and we wind up dead in a ditch."

"Something tells me we'll be ok. So long as that mouth of yours stays good and shut."

Suddenly, Rourke's phone chimed. He pulled it out of his pocket and answered it. "Agent Harken."

"Rourke, it's Director Hollis. Listen carefully."

"What's the situation sir?"

"Parker McCoy's body has gone missing. Stolen right out of the morgue," Hollis said.

"He what," Rourke exclaimed. "When?"

"They only found out yesterday. No idea how long. Someone swapped bodies at the morgue. Jackasses didn't realize they had the wrong corpse until they went to ship it out for cremation."

Ben looked at his partner worriedly. "Rourke?"

Rourke held up a hand. "Do we have any leads, sir?"

"The body left behind was an EMT that went missing after picking up a body from an animal attack. It has a strange mix of drugs in it that we're analyzing now. Have you made any progress looking for McCoy's killer?"

"Arnold Grant is secure, as is Troy Berlin. We're in New Mexico now, about to drive to New Jersey."

"Drive? Why aren't you boys catching a flight?"

"Grant and Berlin have attached themselves to the case without giving us much option. We can't in good conscience fly with Berlin, and we may need both of them if …"

"If what?"

"If the killer is Deacon James."

The other end of the connection was silent.

"Sir?"

"If Deacon James is alive, let alone responsible for this, we aren't going to have the resources necessary to handle this," Hollis said.

"I know sir. Ben's already on top of it. That's why we're bringing these two with us."

"I'm counting on you two. Get to Jersey ASAP. I have some calls to make."

"Yes sir," Rourke said before shutting off his phone and shoving it into his pocket. "Ben, we've got a serious problem."

"What? Rourke, what's going on?"

Rourke motioned for Ben to follow him and he slid into the back seat of the Dodge.

"Troy, I suggest you pin the pedal because we have to get to Jersey on the double," Rourke told them. "I don't mean to alarm anyone but Parker McCoy's body went missing last night."

"Fuck," Troy blurted. "Any idea who..?"

"They don't know. Someone swapped bodies and no one was the wiser. They can't even tell us when exactly it happened."

Arnold and Troy exchanged a look. "We better go. My guess is Deacon had something to do with this," The Crimson Howl guessed.

The Dodge roared to life and sped down the drive, leaving an almost cartoonish cloud of copper-colored dust in its wake. New Jersey was days away and the Agents, along with Troy and Arnold, would have plenty of time to speculate who stole the body of Parker J. McCoy.

CHAPTER SIXTEEN

Rudyard Sinclair was sitting at a small table made of driftwood waiting for his guests to arrive. He looked around the tent he called home. To a customer it looked tiny, the darkened space consisting of a table, three chairs and a few curios hung on the wall to give the room a spooky ambiance the out-of-towners really got a kick out of. In actuality, the tent was much larger with sleeping quarters, a full bathroom, and entire rooms filled with occult paraphernalia and artifacts from long-dead cultures and civilizations. The illusions of the Medallion of Delphi were still just as strong after all these years.

Hanging above his chair was a war hammer given to him by the mayor of Kyoto, Japan. He had helped them fend off some unruly demons preying on children. He could hardly keep track anymore. The hammer, the mayor had said, had been used to fight ghouls during the Warring States Period. Rudyard knew the folklore and had hesitated to take such a weapon from the people of Japan. In the end, though, he decided he'd rather have the priceless bit of Japanese antiquity than the fifty-six million yen he was promised. While his fee had grown over the years, so had his bitterness and cynicism. The hammer above his head, at least, was a reminder of days before the end-less monotony of tourist and their fortunes.

Rudyard waited. His friends were coming. The Medallion had shown him in a dream. They were bringing others. Two men. Federal agents. They were going to ask him questions and he'd supply answers. Probably not the answers they were looking for, but answers just the same.

Rudyard stood up and went over to one of the many shelves on the wall. Spices and herbs and other holistic charms and healing agents were lined up, giving the tent a smell of lavender, cinnamon, and lemongrass. He ran his finger across the items until it rested on a jar of liquid. Inside floated a human ear. The same ear that belonged to his beloved Anthony when they were young and stupid. He took it off the shelf with the greatest of care and caressed it, a feeling of longing swept over him and he was overcome with emotion.

The Medallion of Delphi, which had made him a hero in the intervening years, had never made him rich despite all the money he had been offered for his supernatural assistance. He preferred to receive an artifact or a piece of the floorboard to a haunted house he'd exorcised of evil spirits. In the rare cases his exorbitant fee was honored; he'd make a great show of donating it all to museums, schools, or universities. The thought of taking money from anyone with the intention of keeping it made his throat close in anxiety. The Medallion still hadn't forgiven him for using it for personal gain, and so, the only spirit he longed to see, his Anthony, was forever out of reach.

Rudyard heaved a longing sigh, gave the jar with the ear a tiny kiss before putting it back on the shelf. He saw his reflection in Anthony's jar as he set it down. He didn't look a day over forty. He laughed. It was a bald forty, but the Medallion's magic had treated him well. He felt fine except for the tragic rut his life had become. A life filled with nothing but bored, overfed house-wives wondering if their husbands were fucking the maid or the secretary; or lovesick little townies wondering if little Johnny will stay once the baby was born. Rudyard knew the answers to all of these things and for the most part answered honestly. The weeping or laughing patron would pay him the measly five dollars he charged and leave. The next summer day repeating itself until the customers came in not in waves but a trickle that lasted until Memorial Day weekend and start up again in earnest.

The thought of seeing his old friends made him smile, though there was a twinge of melancholy to it. McCoy was dead and the Agents were coming to question him about Deacon. They were still unsure if their hypothesis was correct, that Deacon had survived getting shot twenty-some-odd years ago and had killed Parker J. McCoy.

Of course, Rudyard knew it was true and would tell the agents as much but that was all he would tell them. Things were in motion now and even he was unsure he could trust the two men coming to pay him a visit. There was so much more to this and he wanted to keep up his end of the bargain.

The Medallion hung on the nail and glowed, giving off a rose-colored hue. In a matter of minutes, he would be reunited with his old friends. The thought of it gave him a chill and set his heart racing like back in the old days when they'd be on a mission.

He'd have to get ready.

He hurried over to his father's old trunk and threw it open. His old costume;

Inside floated a human ear.

a cream-colored tunic, puffy silken pants, a tan cummerbund, and of course, the piece de resistance the turban which completed the ensemble. He gathered up the clothes and dressed hastily. He debated about the brown face makeup for a minute. He decided against it. Times had changed. Arnold and Troy might not have changed, but he would. He wouldn't gamble the future on tired theatrics. The only thing missing was the Medallion around his neck. It was in such close proximity to him that he'd be able to control it without wearing it.

The Swami went back to his table and waited. His friends were only a short walk away.

•••

Rourke was pleasantly surprised at the progress they had made since the storm. When Sandy hit, he was in D.C. and his folks had lost power for nearly a week and a half. They lived on the dry side of Leonardo but came out unscathed except for a couple of torn-off shingles and a collapsed tree in the yard. He saw the boardwalk had been pieced back together and the old roller coaster was gone but Rourke found he didn't miss it as much as he thought he would.

Seagulls were flocked together by a discarded slice of pizza and two were fighting over it. Rourke smiled. Even the birds loved Jersey pie.

"Home, sweet home, huh fellas?" Arnold said.

"I told you it wasn't so bad here," Ben reminded him. "Second weekend in May? It's pretty quiet. Be thankful it isn't Memorial Day. Another two weeks and..."

Troy snorted. "I can only imagine the class of people a place like this attracts."

"Families, mostly, Troy. Good, red-blooded, American, white Christian families. Straight, too. Forgot to mention that," Rourke replied.

"Careful Troy," Arnold said, "kid might kill ya' with that wit of his."

Troy grinned. "Duly noted, Arnold."

They walked down the boardwalk in silence. The only people around were young mothers pushing strollers and joggers and elderly folks out for a stroll. A couple of kids in wet suits were braving the still-chilly Atlantic and trying to catch a wave or two. The smell of fried foods wafted down the boardwalk on salty sea-air currents. Suddenly, Rourke missed Jillian. He'd wanted to bring her down here but never got the chance.

Arnold took a long glance at a girl no more than twenty-five jogging down the boardwalk. "Thank God for yoga pants. Out of every modern invention I've seen, yoga pants never cease to amaze me."

Rourke gagged internally.

"Troy, do you know where exactly Rudyard is?" Ben asked. "The boardwalk is nice and all but we've got serious business to attend to and a body that's missing."

Troy stopped and looked around. He frowned a moment, before waving to one of the old timers sitting on a bench.

"Excuse me, sir?" Troy jogged over to the bench. The graying old timer was wearing a sweatshirt that said: "Restore the Shore".

"Can I help you?" the man asked.

Troy flashed his toothy smile. "I was wondering if you'd be able to help a couple of out-of-towners find something. We're looking for a fortune teller."

"Fortune teller?"

"That's right. See, we're looking for a tent. At least I think it's a tent."

"Mister, what do you wanna go to that place for? It's closed last I heard." The man stood up slowly.

Troy put his hand on the man's shoulder. "We don't want to go there and get our fortunes told; that's a heathen practice. The Lord is very strict about that sort of thing. We're looking to talk to the owner about something else."

"I don't want any trouble, mister."

Troy laughed and pulled out his wad of cash from his pocket and peeled off a twenty. "Just point us in the right direction." He stuffed the money in the man's pocket. The old timer pointed ahead of them.

"I wish I could tell you exactly where, but it's a funny thing. The tent don't stay in the same place sometimes. If it ain't next to Spicey's Cantina, it's next to Kohr's Ice Cream, or sometimes it's on the very end of the boardwalk. No one knows why or wants to know. Place gives us the creeps." The man began to walk away but turned around and said, almost as an afterthought. "Place is cursed, I think. Cursed or blessed. Not a lick of damage to it when that Sandy bitch blew in here. Not a lick."

Troy returned to the others. When he went to point in the direction the old timer had point-ed, there the tent stood.

"I guess Rudyard didn't want us to find it until he was decent," Arnold guessed.

"Nothing about that sodomite is decent, Arnold," Troy snarled.

Rourke could've sworn there was affection in Troy's voice.

"Don't start in on him Troy. It's been a long time since we've seen him and we've got work to do."

Troy said nothing as they approached Rudyard's tent.

"So do we just walk in? There doesn't seem to be a door," Rourke observed.

Ben looked puzzled. "This tent doesn't look big enough to hold more than one person, let alone the four of us plus him."

Rourke opened the flap of the tent and all of them walked in.

The four men heard a voice call out. "Enter all who seek knowledge of the mysteries of the occult!"

Troy groaned. "Oh great. Just as dramatic as ever…"

A brilliant flash of orange light illuminated the candle-lit room, followed by the cracking sound of thunder. Rudyard Sinclair, The Swami stood before them in full regalia, The Medallion of Delphi glowing orange. "Come in! Come in but do not tell me your names." He gestured to Rourke and Ben. "I have dreamed of this moment for a fortnight! A bear and a wolf, a dog, and jackass would be gracing my humble abode." He pointed at Arnold, "The wolf!" He then pointed at Ben, "the bear," then to Rourke, "the dog." And then finally at Troy. His voice went from theatrical and booming to flat, "and the jackass."

"Very funny, Rudyard," Arnold said dryly.

Troy twitched and Rudyard smirked a little.

Rudyard turned to Arnold, opening his arms wide. "Arnold, you look like complete dog shit." He wrapped the Crimson Howl in a tight embrace.

"Why does everyone keep saying that?" Arnold returned the hug, lifting the smaller man off the ground.

Rudyard turned to Troy and the two men looked at each other for a moment. Ben saw contempt in Rudyard's face, his eyes lidded. His expression simmered.

"Troy."

"Rudyard," Troy broke out in a fit of laughter. "My God, it's been too damned long!"

"How are Vera and the babies?" Rudyard, also laughing, wiped a tear from his eye.

"They're fine. Just fine, Rudyard." He slapped his friend on the back. Arnold was smiling and Ben was, too. Rourke simply looked bored.

"Sorry to barge in on you unannounced Rudyard but there's trouble. These two fellas here…" Arnold indicated the agents.

Rudyard silenced him with a wave of his hands. "I said do not tell me their names!" he turned to Rourke and Ben and turned on his show voice, the one he used to use in his old magician days. "I believe a demonstration of my power is in order!"

"Let him have his fun, Troy," Arnold pleaded.

"My goodness," Rudyard began, "such serious-faced young men, and handsome, too! Had I known you were coming I would have done something with the place."

"It's bigger on the inside," Ben puzzled.

"Ah! An Irishman, I love it! Yes, it's bigger on the inside. Or is it?" Rudyard brought his hands together as if he were squeezing a ball between them and the Medallion's color changed from orange to purple.

"Are you seeing this?" Ben asked, his mouth agape.

"Seeing what?" Rourke queried.

"The room's shrinking!"

"The room is the same size, Ben."

Rudyard never wavered. "I see we have a skeptic in our midst. I assure you, young man, I am the genuine article. Please, sit and let me show you."

He snapped his fingers and a table and chairs appeared behind him. "The Swami knows much and sees much. The Medallion of Delphi is a gateway to the other side. Come! Sit both of you and I will prove it to you."

"Mister Sinclair, we really don't have the time, we're on a sensitive mission and..."

"Yes, Parker McCoy is dead and Deacon James killed him. The body has been stolen and you want to know if I had anything to do with it and whether or not Deacon can be stopped. All good things in their own good time, young man. Now sit." Rudyard gestured to the table and chairs. Ben quickly took a seat. Rourke reached out and touched the back of a chair. He could tell Ben was curious. What the hell, Rourke thought. If it meant getting to the bottom of this shit, I'm game.

Rudyard swooped around the room and sat down at the head of the table. He cracked his knuckle. The Medallion of Delphi gave off a white light, like headlights in fog. "Let's see, who to start with. Ah, The Medallion tells me to start with..." his voice trailed off and he pointed at Ben. "You!" Rudyard shouted. He put his fingers in the air and began to wiggle them. He closed his eyes and the Medallion's dim light pulsed. "Mmm-hhmm, yes, it's coming to me. The spirits are lively today."

Rourke looked over at Ben who seemed mesmerized by the display.

"You!" Rudyard pointed at Ben. "You were named after your paternal grandfather. Your parents couldn't decide on a middle name, so they chose Francis after watching a rerun of M*A*S*H, their very favorite TV show. You had a dog named Hawkeye, even. A little King Charles Spaniel, so cute. The dog followed you from Dublin to America, sitting on your lap the entire car ride from Newark Airport. You cried for days when he died."

"How did you...?" Ben gasped.

"Your grandfather is sitting behind me right now. He told me. He told me to tell you he's fine. He knows you miss him and your... oh that's cute, you call her Gram. They're both fine and dandy."

Ben began to tear up. "I...uhm...is... is Hawkeye...?"

Rudyard's voice was warm and comforting. "Oh, Mister Mulcahey you'd be surprised how many people come into my shop and ask about their dead pets. Not their dearly departed husbands or wives, not their grand-ma-ma's or even who they may have been in a past life, no, Ben, a great many people come in wondering if their pets are okay. Touching, really." He paused closed his eyes again and nodded. "He's fine, Benjamin. Just fine. They go to heaven too, you know."

Tears fell from Ben's eyes.

Rourke had seen enough. "Aw, come on, Ben. You don't really believe that. Don't let him get into your head."

"Ah! The skeptic still denies my powers," Rudyard chuckled. "Well, Thomas doubted Christ and they made him a saint. I'm no Jesus, though I've had the pleasure of meeting him. Good Jewish boy. Loves his mother."

Rourke sneered at Rudyard. "Look, it's pretty easy to fool Ben. He looks at you Exceptional people like, I don't know, rock stars. You could have told him his eyes were brown and he'd believe you. You go digging for emotions until you hit nerve, then you work it until it's raw."

"Harry Houdini used to spend a lot of time revealing mediums and psychics as frauds. Boy, you should have seen the look on his face when I found him on the other side. I laughed in his face." Rudyard closed his eyes. "I do not blame you for not believing, Mister Harken. The two of us are bit of a pair. Quite alike."

"I doubt we're alike at all, Mister Sinclair, or do you prefer The Swami?"

"There is a great and unyielding sadness in you. You lost someone very near to you, as I have. It is a grief only widowers share, I'm afraid. An isolation, a bitterness."

Rudyard put his hands up and Rourke noticed the Medallion's glowing pulsations begin again. "Does the name Badger mean anything to you, Rourke?"

Rourke's heart skipped a beat. "What?"

"You had taken her to the zoo one afternoon. She loved going to the zoo. When you came upon the badger exhibit, she thought they were cute. You called her Badger that day and it stuck."

Rourke blinked. "Shut up," he said, barely audible.

"She was beautiful," Rudyard said, casually. "A raven-haired beauty with icy blue eyes but there was nothing cold about her, was there, Rourke?"

"Stop it," Rourke warned, his voice still a whisper.

"She called you John, and you loved her for it. Not even your parents called you by your given first name. Oh, this is interesting," Rudyard flexed his fingers in the air. "She called you Jonathan but only when you made love and she...oh my, she'd bite your shoulder oh so gently when she..." Rudyard opened his eyes, and he looked at Rourke with true pity. "I'm so sorry for your loss. There was such joy in her."

Rourke was breathing heavily and had broken out in a cold sweat. His heart was a thudding jackhammer in his chest. "She's here?"

Rudyard smiled. "Jillian? Oh yes."

"I... I want to see her," Rourke demanded.

"I'm afraid that isn't possible, The Medallion can only be worn by those with the mental fortitude to wield its power. Weak men have tried only to find they either go mad or their brains leak out of their ears. I assure you though, she is here and—"

Rourke drew his gun and pointed it in Rudyard's face. He thumbed back the hammer with an audible click.

Ben's face went white as a sheet. "Rourke put the –"

"NO!" Rourke screamed.

Rourke could barely hear Arnold speaking behind him. "Don't interfere Troy. Let 'em work it out."

Rourke leaned in slowly. "Listen to me, you two-bit Liberace. Give me the Medallion."

Rudyard put his hands up. "Mister Harken it's simply not possible. The Medallion will kill you if you put it on. Please, don't do this."

"Give it to me or I'll shoot that motherfucking turban off your fucking head, do you hear me?"

Rudyard heaved a sigh. "I don't want your death on my conscience, Mister Harken. I already have enough guilt in my life. I know how you feel. I want to see the man I loved all those sunny years ago, but I can't."

Rourke's heart was hammering. "I don't give a shit."

Irritation flashed over Rudyard's face. "Very well, Mister Harken. If you wish to commit suicide right here and now..." He removed his turban revealing his shiny, bald head. "I will oblige you. Don't blame me when your heart explodes or your bowels turn to goo and leak out your asshole." He removed the still pulsating medallion from his neck. "Put out your hand."

"Rourke, no." Ben begged. "Please, don't do this."

"I gotta see her, Ben." Rourke put out his hand and noticed the heat coming off of the Medallion. It throbbed like a living thing with a pulse. Its light surrounded his free hand.

"You've been warned, Mister Harken," was the last thing he heard Rudyard say before he put the Medallion around his neck.

The world stopped. No noise. No movement. The colors drained away, leaving everything in black and white. The lines around people smudged and blurred until everything became a haze of grey. Rourke tried to breathe, but couldn't. The world shifted violently around him, tossing him from his chair. He was drowning.

When Rourke was eleven, he almost drowned in the Atlantic not too far from where Rudyard's tent now stood. He swum out farther than he thought and got caught under a pretty big wave and he went under. Water had filled up his nose and he reflexively coughed and inhaled seawater. His airsupply several feet above him, he panicked and kicked his feet furiously, his head buzzing and dark claustrophobia seeped into him. That feeling of not being able to breathe, of his heart racing and the frantic, animal-like search for air came over him as the Medallion tore through the thin scrim of reality to what Rudyard would call the other side.

•••

Rourke clawed his way through the colorless, noiseless space before a rush of air and the ground striking him. He lay washed ashore on a white beach, the void lapping at his feet. The buzzing in his head stopped, his heart slowed and his mind calmed. He could breathe again. Rourke opened his eyes and there she was, standing over him.

She was smiling, her teeth practically gleaming in the light. That beautiful hair he ran his hands through while she was alive was so close he could smell it. It was honeysuckle on a warm evening. Her beautiful blue eyes that had enchanted him those many years ago glowed with vibrant life.

He stood up quickly, his eyes never leaving her. He wanted to tell her everything. How much he missed her how much he loved her and how much he wanted her. His mind raced. There was so much he wanted to say. How sorry he was she was here and how he wished it had been him and not her who had gotten sick. So much.

"Hi... Badger," his voice was hoarse with emotion.

"Hello, John."

Her voice was as sweet as he remembered. Rourke looked away as he wiped his eyes. They were in her favorite park, he realized, the one just a few blocks away from their apartment. There was a strong scent of cherry blossoms in the cool breeze; the sky was a soft, warm blue that spoke of early summer. It was as beautiful as it was empty.

"Is this... Is this Heaven?"

Jill simply smiled. "I don't know. It's not Hell. I don't suffer here. I haven't seen God if that's what you're wondering, but I don't think it's Purgatory, either." Rourke went to embrace his wife but found himself behind her instead of in her arms. She giggled. "That tickles."

Rourke turned around. "It was worth a shot."

"Walk with me, John. I've missed you." Jill began heading towards the cherry blossom trees and Rourke followed.

They were silent at first. Rourke was still having trouble figuring out what to say to his wife. He wasn't sure how much time he had with her and he wanted to tell her everything but the words wouldn't come out.

"I've been watching you," Jill related. "I can do that now. Being in this place, I can see things."

"That hardly seems fair. I don't even get a warning or a chance to get ready first."

Jill laughed. "What? Worried I'll see that bedhead of yours? You don't need to hide from me." Her expression faltered. "You never apologized to Ben, sweetheart. He was only trying to help after I died. You shouldn't have snapped at him like that."

Rourke's face flushed. He looked down, guiltily. "I know, Badger. It's on my to-do list."

Jill stopped and stepped in front of him. "Do it soon, okay? He thinks about it a lot. He feels bad and I know you do too."

Rourke looked down at his shoes. "I will. I promise."

"John, look at me. You need to be careful. These men... They're dangerous. I can't see everything but something's wrong. Promise me you'll be careful and you'll look after Ben, okay?"

"Jill, we'll be fine. These guys are just windbags who happen to look really good for men in their nineties."

A flash of anger spread across Jill's face. "Promise me!" She reached out to grab him by shoulders, but her hands passed through him. "Damn it."

Rourke wanted to pull her close to him and stroke her hair and assure her he would be fine but that was out of the question. "I promise, Jill. I'll look after Ben, too. I promise."

Jill's eyes welled with tears. "Oh, John. You deserve to be happy, you know that don't you? You spend too much time mourning me that you've forgotten you still have plenty of life to live. There is someone else out there for you."

"Nothin' doing, Badger. There isn't anyone else in Heaven and Earth."

"I love you, John. But you have to go back now."

Rourke's heart sank. "I don't want to."

"I know. We'll see each other again. Some day."

He smiled. "But until then, I guess you'll just have to watch me shower."

"You always knew how to ruin a moment, John." She smiled back.

Rourke reached for the Medallion but paused before touching it. "I love you, too, Jill." He took the Medallion, which still throbbed with an eerie life and removed it from around his neck. The world he inhabited just a few seconds ago faded away into an ether of swirling galaxies and blackness. No suffocation this time, no drowning in the void. Instead, he found himself lying on the floor of Rudyard's tent. He opened his eyes to see not his wife, but Ben standing over him, asking if he was all right. His gun was still in his hand.

"...ya all right?" Ben was saying.

Rourke blinked, had it all been a dream? Had he fainted? The Medallion was in his hand but it had gone cold, its misty white glow had faded to nothing. Rudyard and Ben helped him to his feet.

"Remarkable!" Rudyard marveled. "You put on the Medallion of Delphi and you didn't go crazy and your brains didn't melt. How do you feel?"

"Other than a little woozy, I feel fine."

Rudyard grinned. "I felt the same way when I first wore the Medallion." He held out his hand. "If I may?"

Rourke gave him the Medallion and noticed his gun. "I... er... sorry about this."

"Water under the bridge, young man." He clasped his hands together. "So, you saw her. Now do you believe my power?"

"I do."

Ben smiled.

"Good! Then let us get down to the task at hand, shall we?" He snapped his fingers and two more chairs appeared at the table. "Let's talk."

CHAPTER SEVENTEEN

November 1947
New York, New York

The thing everyone assumes about New York in the 40's is that it was all glitz and glamour and neon lit Art Deco. They picture a metropolis filled with lavish nightclubs, big band music, and high culture. The truth of the matter is The Big Apple, like so many other cities back then, was a hotbed of crime and poverty despite the showiness of Broadway. Tenement houses in Hell's Kitchen and the Bowery still smelled like hot piss; and the whores turning tricks down at the docks were turning up dead at an alarming rate but nobody really cared. After World War Two ended, the country found itself in a post-war boom, but it was an uneven takeoff. The golden ages of the 50s were still a few years away, and The Commission was doing everything it could to maintain its stranglehold.

Of course, the Exceptional People, with their capes, masks, and increasingly elaborate powers were doing what they could to stop it, and, for a while, they succeeded. But the Commission always found a way to even the odds. Pretty soon, the bodies started piling up in what became known as the Superhero War of 1947. The Mafia started paying off supervillains to do their dirty work and throw the Exceptionals off of their trail so they could continue their rackets without being bothered. It was a brilliant strategy that proved wildly successful.

The newspapers had a field day with it; photographers took pictures of even the most gruesome crime scenes. When the Human Torpedo, an Automatic Man wannabe, was found headless and handless at the bottom of the East River, pictures of his bloated corpse graced the front page of every newspaper on the East Coast. Even the heavy hitters like The Crimson Howl and The Automatic Man, fresh from the fight in Europe, were drawn into the seedy gangland violence as soon as they stepped off the boat.

Rudyard read the newspapers every day with growing concern. He lived with his father in a small house in Brooklyn. Bay Ridge had its share of wise guys and hoods, but even though they mostly kept to the Italian Side of 11th Avenue, it worried him. His father told him not to worry, their house in the primarily Hasidic Jewish section of 59th, with only a handful of Italian and Korean families breaking up the neighborhood. Guinea hoods would leave them alone since they had nothing of value. Rudyard didn't argue with his father, even if their house was stuffed full of priceless archaeological finds. No one argued with Professor Sinclair.

Still, the headlines and pictures unnerved him. When he saw the pictures in the newspaper of The Human Torpedo it had given him nightmares for a week. He worried for his father who walked every day to catch the subway to take him into Manhattan. Professor Sinclair was a wiry, mousy man with thick spectacles and a thin moustache. He was nearly bald, save for a heroic comb-over that was light brown but growing grayer. When he was younger, he brought Rudyard with him to various dig sites all over the world. By the time Rudyard was eighteen, he had been to twenty-seven different countries. However, since his father's specialty was Ancient Greece, he spent a great many summers sweating away under the hot, Grecian sun.

Rudyard had taken after his mother, standing taller than Professor Sinclair, with a round, robust face, his green eyes piercing but kind. He had a piano player's long fingers and despite having no aptitude for sports, was trim and fit, sculpted like a statue of Apollo. His looks had gotten him a lot of attention, but never from the gender he cared to give it back to.

Many nights were spent with his head buried in his pillow, soaking it with hot tears. He wondered if his mother had known about his desires and that was why she'd left him and his father. Even though his father wasn't a reactionary man, the thought of telling his father his secret scared him more than anything in the world. Maybe when his father had been Jonathan Sinclair instead of the cold Professor Sinclair he'd become. Rudyard dreamed of his father giving him that look he always gave Rudyard whenever he was upset with him. Not a stern, sharp look, but one of resigned sadness, of profound disappointment. He was giving it from the door of their home as men in white coats dragged Rudyard away to electrocute the pervert out of him.

That, though, was before his father died.

In the early winter of 1947, Professor Sinclair was sent to Egypt to collect artifacts for the museum from a Pharaoh's tomb. When his father was found dead in his tent, the locals said it was the mummy's curse but Rudyard knew it was malaria. Professor Sinclair's body was flown back to New York and cremated. Rudyard had been left a small inheritance and the artifacts left behind were worth quite a bit as well. The prospect of living alone terrified and thrilled him, but there was one thing in particular, now that his father was dead, he could finally have access to.

•••

The Medallion of Delphi was an odd little thing, Professor Sinclair had said, and forbade Rudyard never to go near it. It was the only time Rudyard ever saw his timid father switch from disappointment to anger was when he was fifteen and tried to pick the lock of the trunk to get to the artifact inside. At first, he thought his father was going to strike him, but he didn't. Instead, his mousy father's voice shook with rage. The booming tirade washed over Rudyard, the words crystallizing into a single point; Jonathan Sinclair was afraid. He was terrified of the Medallion of Delphi, of what it could do, and Professor or no, he would never remove it from that trunk. He made Rudyard swear that he would never try to open the trunk again and Rudyard agreed.

With his father dead and ashes, there was no one left to enforce any such agreement. The first thing Rudyard wanted to do was get the key and unlock the trunk, but he decided to wait and do a little research first. His father had several journals he had written in describing his finds over the years. As he combed through his father's writing, he noticed there were only a few words written about the Medallion of Delphi.

In his father's perfect script it read, "Unholy talisman of unspeakable power."

It caused a chill in Rudyard's blood and he snapped the journal shut. He glanced at the trunk and saw the faint green-blue glow beckoning to him. He put the book down and rushed out of the room quickly. Rudyard wouldn't return to it for a week after that.

Being on his own and having a small amount of money meant Rudyard was able to do as he pleased. This meant Rudyard found himself at the library more often than not, researching as much as he could about the Medallion of Delphi. There was nothing to indicate such a thing even existed. The only scrap of a clue came from the mythic history of Greece.

The Oracle of Delphi was able to predict the future and speak with spirits in the Underworld. It was reasoned that The Oracle's "visions" were because of natural gases rising from cracks in the cave. What if, Rudyard wondered, she was able to communicate with spirits because of the medallion his father had found in Delphi?

It seemed like the most logical answer and young Rudyard was pleased with himself. There wasn't anything to fear from an amulet that would let him speak to ghosts. Ouija boards were the stuff of party games and fakirs. He resolved to return home later that day and finally open up the trunk his father had years ago forbidden him to open.

•••

Rudyard's hands trembled as he took the keys out of his father's desk drawer. The trunk was still now; no pulsing blue-green light radiated from it. This steadied Rudyard's quaking hands as he slid the key into the padlock. He turned the key and the lock opened with a hefty "thunk." He slowly removed the padlock and opened the trunk.

It was slightly larger than a half dollar coin and made from what appeared to be silver. Greek writing, pre-Hellenistic from the look of it, was etched deeply on the surface. A modern silver chain lay next to it. Aside from the Medallion, the trunk was completely empty. Rudyard scooped up the Medallion. Despite being made of metal, it was oddly warm to the touch.

"What a piece of junk," he put the Medallion around his neck.

That was a flash of blue-green light and then, Rudyard felt like he was drowning. His lungs cried out for air. His eyes bulged as the colors in his eyes rent themselves apart, bursting into brilliant pale blue light. The color that followed the wash of blue stuck with him, like oil coating them. Rudyard would never be able to capture the words to describe it, no matter how many times he bathed in it.

What he saw after wasn't exactly his home, but it wasn't not his home either. It was his father's study but not as if looking at it through a funhouse mirror out on Coney Island. The room was distorted and ghostly as if a mist had overtaken the entire room. He tried to scream but found his voice had gone.

Rudyard felt his wits leave him; certain something in him had broken as he saw his father standing in front of him as if he were alive and well.

"Unholy!" his father cried, as he reached out to his son. Rudyard, choking and struggling to scream, (reached out to grab his father's hand but they passed through each other, the frost of fear, paralyzing Rudyard's spine. His father screamed and Rudyard's world went black.

•••

He awoke several hours later. The Medallion of Delphi was no longer around his neck but instead clutched tightly in his hand. A dream, Rudyard thought. It was all just a terrible dream. It must have been. His anxiety had caught up to him, that's all. The Medallion was harmless.

Still, he put it back into the trunk and locked it. He left his father's study and locked the door.

•••

In the week following, Rudyard found himself unable to sleep. He would toss and turn, the glow of the medallion looming every time he closed his eyes. As he went about his daily business, it still was ever-present. In the hum of the ceiling fan, the buzz of the refrigerator, the crunch of cereal, he could hear it whispering to him, offering him limitless power. Rudyard did his best to ignore the call, often leaving the house for hours, sometimes days on end. It was easy to do. After all, he was young, free, and had his father's money to spend.

And spend it he surely did.

Rudyard got his first taste of the nightlife while on the run from the medallion. One night, the whispers from the chest echoing loudly in his ears, he took the subway into Manhattan and dove into the first nightclub he could find. It was a spot called The Bowery Club. It was a connected club run by a small-time Mafia hood named Primo Marinelli. Primo was feared in this section of Manhattan because his cousin was the top enforcer for the Bonnano Crime Family. Primo, whose closest associates called him "Number One", ran a very tight ship. That was mostly because everyone from the waiters to the showgirls to the negro porters were terrified of the olive-skinned Sicilian with the sharp Roman nose and slicked black hair and dull, brown eyes. If you saw a busboy with a black eye, they'd been turning tables too slowly. If you peeked into the dressing room, you'd see a showgirl or two doubled over in pain from arriving late to work. Always in the stomach with the talent, Primo would solemnly intone. No bruising on the show ponies. He treated the Negro porters the worst, though, often slapping them around in the front of the house and

...a small time hood named Primo Marinelli...

docking an entire day's pay on top of it for disturbing the guests. Fear kept the gears turning and the club was a hotspot. Rudyard found himself there almost every night, drinking champagne and enjoying himself.

Until the money ran out.

Being young as he was, and with no parents to guide him, Rudyard found himself piss broke after only four months on his own. After months in a drunken stupor, it was a sobering wakeup call. Despite the treasures his father had kept in his study (which he had no idea how to sell) he would need a job, and quick. The postwar recession made it hard for him to find a job anywhere, even the GI's coming home from Europe were having a tough time and if they were having no luck, what chance did Rudyard have?

As he laid awake worried sick about how he'd make money to pay for food and to keep the lights on, he heard the Medallion whispering to him again in the dead of night. He would bury his head in his pillow, wrapping up in his blanket like a cocoon. It wouldn't be until he got his first late notice on the electric bill that he decided he'd give in.

Rudyard unlocked the door to his father's study. Now the blue-green light was so bright it drenched the room in its light, exterminating nearly all the darkness. Sweat ran down Rudyard's face and his heart echoed in his ears. He unlocked the trunk and a surge of warmth washed him in the warm glow of the Medallion of Delphi. This time, his hands were steady as he picked it up from the trunk and placed it around his neck.

He expected the drowning feeling again, the feeling as if his head was about to burst but this time the Medallion was gentler with him. The room once more looked like it was surrounded by a fine mist, but his dead father was nowhere to be found.

There was a woman standing in front of him.

She radiated a pale, blue light. Her features hidden by a thin veil. Rudyard couldn't tell whether it was silk or if it was real at all. What he could make out of her face was that her pupil-less eyes were black. Not brown, but black like a starless sky. She wore a white toga and a laurel of ivy leaves sat atop her veiled head. Her skin was white but not pale; Rudyard's mind spun for the right word. Porcelain? Alabaster? Her lips were thin, her face expressionless.

"Who are you!?" Rudyard cried, his voice sounded distant, like talking into a wind tunnel.

The woman set her black, expressionless gaze on Rudyard. "I am," her words echoing in Rudyard's brain. She did not speak with her mouth, "the Oracle of Delphi."

"Why are you here?" Rudyard stammered,

"Because the Medallion has found you worthy."

"Worthy? What…what do you mean?"

Her thin lips curled into what Rudyard assumed was a smile, despite her frozen features. "There is much I must teach you and my time is short. If you are to wield the Medallion's power, we must begin right away." She approached him slowly, her feet leaving the ground slightly. She hovered to him and Rudyard fell backward. "Do not fear me, boy." But Rudyard was afraid and regretted putting the Medallion around his neck for a second time.

"Please…" Rudyard's voice failed him and it came out as a choked grunt.

The Oracle reached out and placed her hand on Rudyard's shoulder. He could feel her hand, warm and soft, on his shoulder. It was strangely comforting.

"I… I can feel you," he mumbled. "You're not a ghost?"

The Oracle smiled. "I am and I am not. Stand up, boy."

Rudyard stood up. "Why are you here? Why does my father's study look like this?" The room looked as if a fine blanket of mist had covered it as it had when he first put on the Medallion.

"All of this will be revealed in time, Rudyard Sinclair. Now we must go."

Rudyard felt a sense of dread creep down his spine. "Go?"

The Oracle stretched her arm out to her side. The door to the study flung open. Rudyard looked in horror as the hallway leading to the small den was replaced with the swirling of stars. She reached over with her other hand, beckoning him to take it.

Against his better nature, against everything his mind was telling him, the screaming alarm bells ringing in his entire body, he took the Oracle's warm, soft hand and the two of them departed the ethereally misty study into the unknown void the Medallion had seemingly conjured.

•••

Rudyard clutched the Oracle of Delphi's hand with a grip so tight he thought he would crush the woman's delicate fingers. There was no ground beneath them, just miles and miles of nebulae and space as far as his eyes could see and his mind could comprehend. Neither of them fell or floated away but remained fixed in place.

Wide-eyed and full of wonder, Rudyard felt his terror dissipate. The swirling clouds and galaxies were almost hypnotic in their dead silence.

"Where are we?" He asked. He expected his words to echo in the silence but they came out flat and dull. He turned and looked at the Oracle noticing she looked different here. Her eyes were a rich brown, her skin olive; thick black hair draped her petite shoulders. He knew her now from a hundred dig sites, unmistakably Mediterranean. Her eyes read the recognition in Rudyard's face and a warm smile creased her features. A glow spread through Rudyard.

"We are in the walls between time and space." Her voice radiated the same warmth as her smile, even as felt colorless in this star-flecked world. "Do not be afraid of this place. You are safe here."

"Good, because I have a fear of high places," he confessed. The "good" started with a confident tone but by "high places," he could hear his flat voice straining into a whimpered whisper. "I have so many questions."

"And I have answers, Rudyard Sinclair. What knowledge do you seek from the Oracle of Delphi?"

The first question was the most obvious, the easiest to explain (he hoped,) "You said the Medallion chose me."

She nodded.

"Why? What does it mean?"

"Something inside of you, perhaps. A purity or…a rage."

The answer was not what he was expecting at all.

"After the gods defeated the Titans. Hades, god of the underworld, forged the Medallion as a way to observe the Old Gods as they lie in their astral prisons. Zeus coveted the Medallion, as he coveted all relics of great power forged by gods other than himself and set about to retrieve it from his brother. There was a great war and the Medallion was sent from Mount Olympus by Hermes to the mortal realm where it was discovered by the first Oracle."

"You weren't the first?"

"I was the last," she said sadly. "As Greece fell to decadence and into antiquity it was my duty to preserve the Medallion. To keep it safe."

"My father found it buried under thousands of years of stone and dirt," Rudyard recalled. "My tomb." For the first time, her voice was cold. "I was not pleased my resting place was disturbed so." She began to walk and beckoned Rudyard to come with her. He was hesitant at first and took a precautionary small step. He didn't fall into the void but felt his feet firmly planted on something solid despite there being nothing holding him up. By the time he was a bit more surefooted, the Oracle was several paces in front of him. He had to hurry to catch up.

"The Medallion of Delphi is a powerful thing," she continued. "It's a relic of great and terrible power. Only those worthy of it can wear it and wield its might."

"And it chose me, but you don't know why?"

"As I said, The Medallion chooses who it wishes. Sometimes it is a person with a kind heart or compassionate soul, other times it feeds on hot-blooded rage. Several Oracles were chosen throughout the ages because my nation was in the throes of war. They would become trusted advisors to generals. Their divinations would almost always assure victory."

"Almost?"

"The one thing it could not predict was the downfall of our empire," she elaborated. "At first it was used as a weapon, to predict the outcomes of battles, but as the empire grew fat and prosperous the Oracles were no longer needed. We went from palaces to living in caves, telling fortunes to wealthy Greek women. Such a tremendous power in such a small thing wasted on overfed harpies." The Oracle despaired.

"What kind of power?"

"The power to see the future and the past. To see the realm of spirits, of those who reside between the mortal life and the spiritual plane. The wearer can hold communion with gods and demons, monsters and otherworldly creatures. Those who hide in the shadows and those whose mortal eyes cannot see. The Medallion pulls the veil back upon reality itself."

"The supernatural," Rudyard whispered.

"That is what you call it in your time?"

"Yes," Rudyard agreed. "That was why I could see my dead father when I first put it around my neck? That's why the room looked like it was filled with mist?"

"Your insight is correct. When an Oracle dies, a new one takes its place. The previous Oracle reveals the secrets of the Medallion's power. I will show you all I know and more. The power to cast spells, to send a restless spirit to the afterlife in peace, to show a man's true face, to predict the future."

Rudyard's head was swimming. "I could be the most powerful man on earth."

"You could try. Selfish men have before, all have failed. Magic is not to be taken lightly, boy."

"Then I could be rich, at least."

"The Medallion has been used in such ways, but there is always a cost. It is best to use the knowledge and power I give you in more benevolent ways. To aid and comfort the sick, to settle angry spirits. I sense there is goodness in you, boy. I also sense a darkness. You will have to walk a fine line between the two if you are to wield this power I give you responsibly."

Rudyard said nothing for a long time. A part of him wanted to take the Medallion off and throw it into the endless void he now found himself in. What good was power if you couldn't gain anything from it? His inheritance had run out and soon he wouldn't be able to feed himself or keep the lights on in his house. Another part of him wanted to learn what the Oracle had to offer him. There were, after all, exceptions to the rules.

"I am ready to learn what you have to teach me."

The Oracle of Delphi approved. "Then let us begin at once."

Rudyard was content. Once she was done teaching him, he would be the new Oracle, the new wielder of the Medallion, and no musty ghost would stop him from using this part of his inheritance just like he had the rest of it.

•••

The Bowery Club was popular for many reasons, not the least of which was the exciting nightly entertainment attractions that appeared there. Famous singers and dancers would perform all night and vaudeville comedians would bring down the house with their raunchy material, but the performer most, if not all, the people came to see was a scrawny kid in a turban and brown face who called himself the Swami. He was billed as a top-notch illusionist, making doves appear out of thin air and performing levitation tricks so real it caused a panic.

He would tell people's fortunes – lies of course. He would delight audiences by doing simple card tricks, and even making himself appear in two places at once. No one suspected a thing. Rudyard would smile broadly as the audience roared applause and "ohhed" and "ahhed" at his magic tricks.

Anthony would smile, too.

Anthony was a stagehand, a few years older than Rudyard and handsome in a traditional Italian way. Soft, brown eyes and a thick head of black hair. He was tall for a Sicilian at an even six feet and muscular. His complexion was fairer than the dagoes always coming and going in the place. Rudyard teased him about it constantly but was never mean.

Anthony smiled and Rudyard wanted him. His pulse quickened and he suddenly needed to leave. He was sure Anthony would never be his and he could never tell him how badly he wanted him, until the day Anthony surprised him in the alley with a kiss. It was the happiest night of Rudyard's life. He took Anthony back to his house and they made love for the first time. Anthony was rough at first, his passion getting the better of him but he finished gently.

"I've wanted this since the day we met," Rudyard admitted with Anthony's head on his chest. He ran his fingers through his hair. "But I was afraid."

"I wanted you, too." Anthony echoed. There was a very long silence between them. "No one can know."

Rudyard knew it was true. They would have to keep their romance a secret. It wasn't fair and it wasn't right but he knew the way most people felt about what they were doing. He didn't want Anthony to lose his job or to get hurt.

"We could run away, you know," Rudyard suggested. "We don't have to stay here."

Anthony looked up at him. "I left Italy for a better life in America. I like New York. I like my job."

Rudyard conceded. "It was just a thought."

•••

One afternoon he was drinking at the bar of the Bowery Club and heard Primo ranting and raving to Mr. Torelli, his second in command, about how despite doing great business, he was losing money. His uncle needed a bigger kickback because the Super Villains were asking for more money.

"Now I gotta give him thirty percent of the house take so they can hire these costumed cocksuckers," he raged. "A fuckin' dozen Tommy guns and some dynamite would take care of the whole bunch!"

Rudyard was feeling braver than normal thanks to the three whiskey sours he'd consumed. "I may be able to help you."

"The fuck you doin' listening to my conversation? And what the hell are you doing here so early? You ain't on until eight."

"I still get a little jittery before a show. I digress. I believe I can help you."

Primo grabbed Rudyard by the lapels of his suit jacket. "You listen to me you little strunz! If you wasn't my top talent I'd belt you one for talkin' to me like …"

Nonplussed, Rudyard interrupted. "Are you a gambling man, Mister Marinelli?"

"Yeah. So what?"

"What if I told you I could predict the winner of tomorrow's horse race?"

"I'd say you were wasting my fuckin' time."

Primo unclenched his fist and turned to Torelli, "He says he thinks he can help us."

"I don't see how," Torelli said.

Rudyard took a big sip of his whiskey sour. "I was telling Primo that I can predict the winners of the horse race tomorrow afternoon."

Torelli squinted his eyes. "How do you figure you're gonna do that, kid?"

"I am a magician, Mister Torelli, and a magician never reveals his secrets."

"You're drunk," Primo pointed out.

"I'm tipsy. Not drunk. And I can help you. Observe."

He took a pencil from his coat pocket and started writing on a bar napkin. In a minute he had written the names of the horses who would come in first, second, and third in the race at Belmont the following day. The Medallion showed him the winners as clear as if he witnessed the race in person.

"This don't mean shit." Primo groused. "They could lose."

Rudyard merely smiled. "Which is why you aren't going to bet tomorrow. This is a show of trust. If the horses come in as they are written on that napkin tomorrow, you and I can talk about how we can help each other."

"You got a guy on the inside or somethin'?" Primo asked.

"No. Just a very strong gut feeling."

Torelli looked at his watch. "We gotta go, Primo. We got that thing."

"Yeah, alright." Primo looked at Rudyard. "A gut feeling, huh?"

"A very strong gut feeling, Number One." Rudyard raised his glass and gave a wink.

Primo dismissed it and walked out of the club, Mister Torelli waddling quickly behind him.

Anthony surprised him with a brief, yet passionate kiss.

"What was that for?" Rudyard whispered.

"No reason." He paused, his face blushed. "Rudyard, I have to tell you something."

Rudyard's heart sank. A coldness crept into his stomach. A million thoughts ran through his head. He began to take mental inventory of every dumb thing he had said to Anthony over the past half a year, every dumb Italian joke he said and all the times he had been too tired to be cheerful or selfish in bed.

"What?"

"These past few months have been..." he began, "bellissimo."

Rudyard's heart sank even further, he was about to be kicked to the curb. Anthony took his hand.

"What I'm trying to say, you know my English ain't so good sometimes, is that..." He took a deep breath, "Is that... I love you."

Rudyard blinked. "What?"

"I said, I love you. I've never felt this way before. With you, I can be who I really am. When I'm with you, I am so very happy."

Rudyard stood, mouth slightly ajar.

"You don't feel the same?"

Rudyard leaned in and kissed him. He ran his hands through Anthony's dark hair. "I love you, too. I'm going to make all of our dreams come true."

●●●

"I don't know how you did it, kid, but I gotta say, you fuckin' did it!"

"I take it the horses came in as I said they would?" Rudyard grinned already knowing the answer.

"Down to the last nag."

"Good. I hope now you trust me enough to let me pick the winners for the next race."

"Let's not go that far yet, kid. My old man used to say that if something is too good to be true then it probably is. Could have been just a really lucky coincidence."

"I completely respect your skepticism, of course, but I assure you the next race, if you decide to bet on who I pick will be extremely lucrative for you." He reached into his coat pocket and pulled out a small wad of bills. "This represents my entire life savings, nine hundred bucks. I'm gonna put it all on the winning horse. You don't have to bet if you still don't trust me, but I assure you, next week I'll have tripled my earnings."

"Tell me something, kid. If you know who is gonna win the race, why bother telling me? What's in it for you?"

"I only have nine hundred dollars, but you have ninety thousand. If you put up your money and we win, which I guarantee, I only want a small piece of the action."

"How small a piece are we talkin'?"

"Fifteen percent."

"Fuck you."

"Twelve percent," Rudyard adjusted.

"Try six percent, and you'd be lucky to get it."

"I suppose six percent on an ever-increasing scale wouldn't be so bad."

"We'll see on that six percent," Primo cautioned. "I ain't committed to it yet. Besides, you gotta prove this first time wasn't no fluke occurrence."

"Of course. The Swami will deliver what he promises."

•••

Rudyard came back a week later with double his life savings. That cinched it for Primo. He would trust the kid who could call the horses. He offered Rudyard the six percent, as he said he would, but being the type of guy who is well connected and runs a semi-reputable business; scruples were never his strong point. Sure, he'd start out at six percent but the second real dough came in off these bets he'd have to renegotiate with the kid. Of course, Rudyard wouldn't be a part of the negotiations but that's how these things went. The Swami would just have to live with it. He was, after all, on Primo's payroll.

There weren't many big races coming up, the Kentucky Derby wasn't for another few weeks but the fights at the Garden were always a good source of action. He mentioned this to Rudyard who said he'd be delighted to predict the outcome of those fights.

•••

The money started really flowing in the next few weeks. Rudyard was able to predict the winners of every horse race, boxing match, and baseball game worth big money. As the money came in, Rudyard's cut got smaller and smaller.

"This envelope is light," Rudyard commented angrily. "There should be three grand in here."

"My uncle, he needs the money," Primo lied. "I'll get you the rest next week."

"You said that last week, and the week before."

"And I'll keep saying it until you get it through your fuckin' head."

"You guinea fuck." He stared at Primo through narrow eyes. "I know you have that money locked in that safe over there." He pointed to the wall behind him. "By my count you owe me six thousand dollars total."

"Now you listen to me you little..."

Rudyard could feel the heat coming from the Medallion of Delphi. He could have done a number of things, not least of which could have been just making Primo give him the money but he ignored the Medallion's call.

"No, I suggest you listen, Mister Marinelli. We agreed on the paltry sum of six percent and you've been chiseling your way out of giving me my fair cut for weeks now. If I can tell you who's going to win tomorrow's horse race what makes you think I don't know how to crack that safe open and take my share and then some?"

Primo's eyes darted from Rudyard to his safe. It never occurred to him that Rudyard would do something like that. It never occurred to him that anyone would. He couldn't put his finger on it, but suddenly his neck hairs stood up and he felt a chill. No, better to leave this angry young man alone.

He said nothing and went to the wall safe and removed six stacks of hundred-dollar-bills. He threw them on the floor near Rudyard's feet.

Rudyard picked up the wads of cash and stuffed them in his jacket pocket. "I knew you could be reasonable, Mister Marinelli. Now if you'd excuse me, I have to prepare for tonight's performance."

•••

Rudyard looked at his watch. Anthony said nine o'clock and it was already a quarter past. It wasn't like him to be late and Rudyard was starting to worry. He went into the parlor and called the operator.

"Can I have BR5-6221 please?"

The phone rang and rang but Anthony didn't answer.

Cursing, Rudyard went over to the table, sat down, and poured himself a glass of Bordeaux. He took a long swig, not tasting the subtle nuances.

There was a knock at the door.

Rudyard sprang from his chair. He unlocked the door and saw that it wasn't Anthony but someone he had never met holding an envelope, dripping red. In the other hand, he held a gun.

"Primo says come with me. You may look inside the envelope first." He shoved the

envelope at Rudyard.

Rudyard's pulse raced. Slowly, he took the dripping envelope from the man's gloved hand and opened it, a dark dread spreading across his chest.

In it was an ear.

He deduced Primo had grabbed Anthony and hurt him. He dropped the envelope, recoiling in horror and disgust. He was too shocked to speak, his mind spinning too quickly to even think to try to get to the Medallion of Delphi. The gunman pulled the hammer back on his piece as if to remind Rudyard he'd have no trouble using it if he didn't do exactly as he was told.

"Get goin, fruitcake," the gunman ordered. "Primo ain't got all night."

Rudyard didn't think he'd be able to walk. Somehow, he managed to walk out the door, the gunman behind him, the snub-nose of the gun pressing in his lower back. Out on the street, an unmarked black Ford waited.

•••

Primo smiled. He looked at the whimpering young man tied to a chair, a handkerchief gag keeping him silent. Primo insisted on chains. The kid's ear was still bleeding, but in a few minutes, it wouldn't matter.

"I hope you know why this is happening to you," Primo said as the young man moaned in despair. "It's bad enough that little shit Rudyard disrespected me in my place of business, but I have to find out I got a couple of fags working for me, too? Marrone!" Primo spit on the ground. "I want you to know I got nothin' against you, kid. This is business. That sawed-off little cock-sucker needs to be taught a lesson he don't forget."

Torelli approached him. "They're here, Primo."

"Good. Now the fun can begin."

The Ford pulled up and the headlamps shined on the scene. The door flung open and Rudyard was forcefully exited from it. Scrambling to his feet, he tried to run towards Anthony.

"Anthony," he cried, but Torelli met him with a punch to the gut that took the wind out of him. He fell to his knees.

"Look at him," Primo chuckled. "A position he's probably very fond of." Torelli and the gunman laughed. "Or is it the other way around? Who sucks whose cock in that relationship of yours?" He reached into his pocket and pulled out a cigar.

Rudyard realized Primo was going to kill them both and it was all his fault. The Oracle had warned him. He was haughty, he was prideful, he was stupid. The Medallion gave him confidence and power but it had come at a cost. Like the Oracle said it would.

"You know," Primo lit his cigar. "For a little while there, I actually liked you. We had a good thing going. You call the races, I make money and you take what I give you. Had you just kept your fuckin' mouth shut you'd be lickin' your friend's pole right now."

Rudyard looked up at Primo and saw that he was smiling.

"Instead, you chose to insult me, to threaten me in my club, my place of business. Stand up."

Rudyard stood up slowly.

"Now, I've been thinking about it, and I really would like things to go back to normal between us. See, I liked our little arrangement and I really don't want to have to kill you but I can't let a transgression such as what transpired between us go. What kind of businessman would I be if I did such a thing? So I'll make a deal with you."

"A deal?"

"Sure. We can all go home tonight, your little friend too, if you tell me who is going to win the race tomorrow."

"That's all?"

"That's all. You tell me who wins the race tomorrow, or I get you a matching pair of shoes like your boyfriend has and the two of you spend the next sixty years at the bottom of the fuckin' river batting eyelashes at each other till the fish bite them off."

He turned to Torelli. "You think fishes like the taste of queers?"

Torelli shrugged.

"No matter. If you tell me who wins tomorrow, I let him go. I'll even have his ear reattached."

"You... want to know right now?"

"Of course, I wanna know right now."

Normally, the Medallion would show him, but it was at home and he had no idea who was racing tomorrow. Rudyard looked at Anthony. He could see he was crying and his face was wet with blood. His ear was lying on the floor of Rudyard's house. For the first time since he put on the Medallion, he felt completely helpless.

He looked down at the ground. "I... I don't know."

"You don't know?"

Rudyard began to cry. "No. I don't know who is going to win."

"Now, how is it you knew the winner of all those races and all those fights and ball games but now, when your life and the life of the guy who's cock you've been suckin' is on the line you don't know a thing?"

Rudyard said nothing.

Primo turned to Torelli. "Get rid of the kid."

"No!" Rudyard tried to run towards Anthony but this time Primo punched him in the stomach. He fell to his knees again, gasping for breath. Primo moved behind Rudyard and grabbed his head and held it in place.

"Watch," Primo shouted.

Torelli moved quickly, lifting the cinderblock deftly. With a grunt, he tossed it into the water.

Anthony cried out as the chain ran out of links and dragged him down into the river.

"NO!" Rudyard yelled. He managed to free himself of Primo's grip and ran towards the end of the dock.

"Get him!" Primo screamed.

The gunman pulled the hammer back on his gun and fired. Rudyard went down and he once again found himself surrounded by darkness.

•••

He didn't realize it, but he let out a moan.

His eyes opened and all he could feel was a fiery pain between his shoulder blades. The room was white and he was connected to an IV. A glass bottle of clear liquid dripped down the tube.

"You're finally awake."

Rudyard didn't recognize the voice and was too weak to even look around to see who said it.

The figure belonging to the voice came into his line of sight. He was a negro, not too tall, his hair slightly gray.

"My name is Doctor Parker McCoy. Rest easy, son. You've had a busy day."

Rudyard was still disoriented. "Where...?"

"In the hospital. Two of my associates found you in the nick of time."

"Anthony?"

Parker's head dropped. "Afraid he didn't make it."

Rudyard closed his eyes, tears rolled down his cheeks.

"As I was saying. Two of my associates found you while on patrol. A good thing, too, since you were bleeding to death right there on the dock. My guess is Marinelli heard them coming and left you there before he had a chance to finish the job."

Rudyard's eyes opened. They were bloodshot. "Marinelli."

"He's still alive, Mister Sinclair. I've been watching you for a while now. Heard you were the best magician in New York. I could use a man of our talents."

"What are you... talking about?"

"Of course, you have to tell me how you do those illusions of yours. I know a magician isn't supposed to reveal his secrets but let's just say if you tell me, I'll help you get revenge on those guinea hoods that killed Anthony."

For a moment Rudyard looked at the ceiling. He had survived but had lost everything he held dear. He had chanced fate and didn't heed the Oracle's advice about abusing his power. Now Anthony was dead. He had abused his power, and he would never let that happen again.

"It's not a trick."

"What's that?" McCoy asked. "What'd you say?"

"The illusions were real. It comes from the Medallion."

"Impossible."

"Nothing is impossible, Doctor McCoy. The Medallion of Delphi showed me that."

McCoy stood up and pulled a card from his pocket. "This is an address I want you to visit in D.C. when you are well." He put it on Rudyard's bed, "When you want to talk some sense drop by. My associates are looking forward to meeting you."

"If I show you the Medallion, will you help me get Marinelli?"

"I'm not the type of guy who gets his hands dirty. The guys who saved you, they're the types of guys who get their hands dirty."

"And who might they be?"

McCoy smiled. "Why, The Crimson Howl and The Automatic Man, of course."

"Tell them thanks, but I'll handle it myself."

•••

The picture of the corpse of Primo Marinelli was in every major newspaper on the East Coast and even made it all the way into the Los Angeles Times. His body was discovered in the alley behind The Bowery Club. No foul play was suspected and the coroner ruled his death a heart attack but Torelli knew better. Nobody's hair turns white like that because they have a little heart trouble. Primo confided in him a few weeks before he died that weird things were happening to him. Strange things, like seeing that kid they threw into the drink from the corner of his eye but when he'd turn his head the kid would be gone.

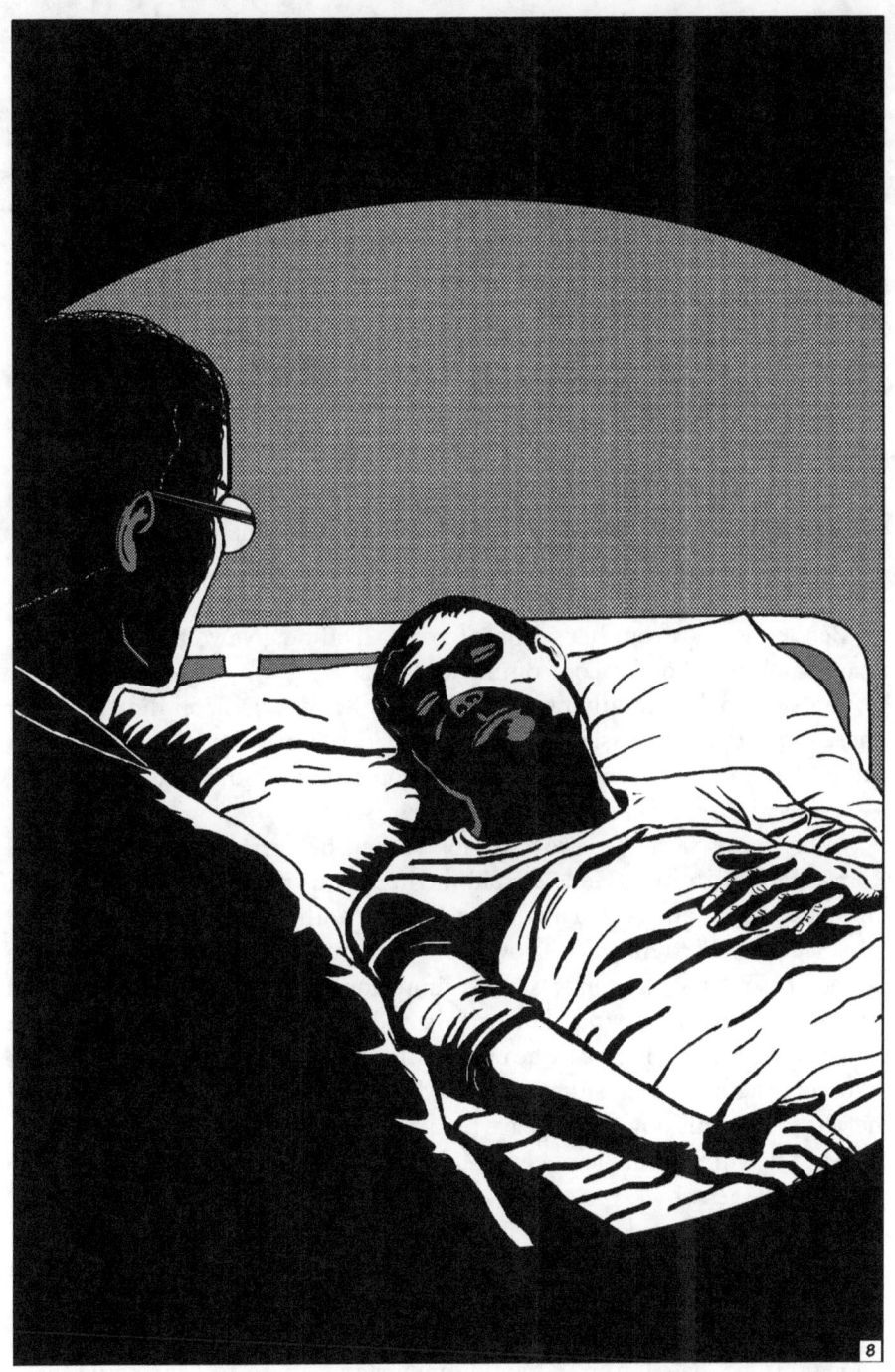

"Nothing is impossible, Doctor McCoy."

Primo never confessed the nightmares he'd been having though. The way he'd wake up screaming bloody murder at night. It had gotten so bad that Primo had stopped sleeping the two weeks before he died. He'd spent most of his time at the club, hiding in his office from the night terrors and the kid whom he saw out of the corner of his eye. His heart finally gave out when he was taking out the trash in the middle of the night and the bloated, earless, crab-eaten corpse of the kid they'd thrown in the river sprang from the dumpster.

Of course, there was no corpse. It was merely Rudyard Sinclair, The Swami, getting his sweet, sweet revenge.

CHAPTER EIGHTEEN

"That is how I met Parker McCoy, Agents," Rudyard finished. "It was an experience that defined our relationship. He put me in contact with my current companions and built our team, but he and I never seemed to gel the way he did with Troy or Arnold."

Ben looked up from his scribbled notes. "Did he give you any indication that he was afraid of Deacon coming for him?"

Rudyard looked mildly offended. "Never. Besides, Deacon didn't murder those men. The alien inside of him did. Deacon James the man and Deacon James the superhero were very different people, Agent Mulcahey."

"What was the difference, then?" Rourke asked.

"When he first started working for Parker, he carried a Crimson Howl comic book with him. He later told me he was inspired by what he saw on those pages. The alien mold made a sort of deal with him when it latched on to him. He'd receive tremendous power, but in return, he would have to consume human flesh. Now, Deacon was half a simpleton when he discovered the mold in a meteor, but even a simpleton understands you simply do not eat people."

Troy spoke up. "That's why he only ate the men we were tracking. Maybe he figured it was a win-win situation. The whatever-it-is gets his people meat and he gets to keep his powers and save regular people."

Arnold grunted in agreement. "Makes a shit-ton of sense to me. What do you think, Agents?"

"It's as good an explanation as any," Ben decided. "But it begs the question as to why he decided to take a bite out of Dr. McCoy. Rudyard, did Deacon ever give any indication that he harbored animosity or ill will towards McCoy?"

"In all the years I knew Deacon, he never told me he didn't like McCoy. Though if he hated him, I could understand that. McCoy could be a condescending prick when he wanted to be."

"Watch your mouth, Rudy. That's our friend you're talking about," Troy retorted.

Rudyard sneered. "Your friend, Troy. He was no friend to me. Just a guy I worked for. We were all just guys who got their hands dirty for the great genius Parker J. McCoy and nothing more." There was a cold bitterness in his voice. He turned his gaze back to the two agents. "Let me tell you a little something about the Golden Age that isn't in your files or history books or in Arnold's autobiography.

"Agents, the Golden Age was a sham. It really was. It's the truth, Troy! It was all a scam and Parker McCoy was the mastermind behind the whole thing. He was probably the most powerful man in the world by 1955."

Ben's eyes widened. "Go on."

Rudyard continued. "No one can take away just how incredibly smart Parker was. He was ten times the genius of Einstein, but his true power was how persuasive he could be. He was able to bend people to his will. He had a way of speaking that could just... convince you. Hitler had a similar way if you study the history."

"Now see here, Rudyard. McCoy wasn't always a nice fella, but he wasn't no Hitler," Arnold argued.

"Maybe not, but tell that to the people in Harlem we had to knock around." Rudyard turned to Ben and Rourke. "All those people wanted was a better neighborhood, to be treated the same as white folks but instead of better schools and better housing they sent us in to crack skulls. That was all McCoy."

Troy's eye twitched a little. "Why the hell would a black man want us to hurt other black people, Rudyard, if they weren't breaking the law?"

"Protesting in the street isn't breaking the law."

Rourke wasn't having it. "Rudyard, that doesn't really answer our question. Did Deacon want to kill McCoy? I can understand why you might have felt a certain way about him, but you didn't bite into his abdomen. Deacon clearly did."

"Yes, I suppose you're right. I apologize. It's hard remembering the old days, Agent Harken. We were supposed to be superheroes, not government attack dogs. Deacon never mentioned wanting to kill him, no. In fact, when Deacon started getting the itch, he went to McCoy for help before telling the rest of us."

Ben leaned forward. "Did he ever tell you what McCoy did to help him?"

"Yes. McCoy devised some kind of chemical injection that would suppress his desire to eat people, as gruesome as that sounds to say out loud. It worked for a while."

"Not long enough, though," Arnold added. "See, even after the injections he still ate people. This time, innocent people."

"Were they really innocent?" Troy countered. "How do we know it wasn't a setup to get Deacon killed? Some former supervillain could have—"

Rudyard waved his hand again. "Don't be so naïve, Troy. By the time Deacon started killing those people, most of the villains had retired or were rotting in jail. Why did Deacon kill McCoy? I honestly don't know, Agents." He looked a bit defeated. "Maybe the pan-galactic space mucus wanted him dead for supplying Deacon with the stuff to suppress his appetite."

"So there really is no motive here. Just guessing in the dark. It could be a million different reasons," Rourke surmised.

Rudyard nodded slowly. "I'm afraid so, Agents. I wish I could be of more help to you."

"Do you have any idea where he may be hiding?" Ben asked. "Since you knew him best would you where he might go?"

Rudyard thought for a moment. "He always talked about going back to his mother's house. It was demolished back in seventy-eight or nine. If he was sad about it, he never said. He wasn't good at expressing emotion."

"That was in... Waterbury, Vermont?" Rourke recalled from the files.

"Brattleboro," Rudyard corrected. "He lived there until he was twenty-two, I think. He worked for a short time at the Brattleboro Asylum. It's called the Brattleboro Retreat now."

"When he was shot back in the nineties it was in the gazebo of a park near the Retreat, right?" Rourke wanted confirmation.

"It was."

"So, he kills innocent people and goes back home to Brattleboro."

"Supposedly innocent," Troy once again objected.

Rourke shot him a look. "So, he kills supposedly innocent people and goes home, gets shot in the back but it doesn't actually kill him, but there are no records of him being sent to the county morgue or even buried. McCoy gets killed the same way the supposedly innocent people do and he runs off again, but not before writing 'Find Howl' on McCoy's wall. We get called in to investigate and go out to L.A. to find Arnold safe and sound. None of this makes any sense."

"If he went home after he killed them people, he could be following a pattern," Arnold proposed.

"But why write he was trying to find you, then turn and head north instead of west?"

Ben followed up. "Unless it wasn't him that was looking for Arnold. Maybe he wanted us to go get him. Maybe the message wasn't of intent but instruction." Ben put his hands on his head and leaned back in the chair. "Maybe he's been setting this all up from day one. Look around you, Rourke. With the exception of McCoy, all of Deacon's former friends are in one place. Maybe he wants us to go to Brattleboro to confront him."

Troy and Arnold exchanged looks. "That still doesn't take into account who stole McCoy's body," Troy reminded them.

Rourke's cell phone trilled. He checked the screen. "It's Director Hollis."

"Yes, sir?" he said.

"Rourke? This is very important. Who is with you right now?"

"Ben and I are here wrapping up our interview with Rudyard Sinclair. Troy and Arnold are with us as well."

"Good. You're going to need them. Put me on speakerphone." Rourke obliged. Hollis' voice crackled with static. "What I'm about to say goes no farther than present company. Understood?"

"Absolutely," Rourke answered.

"I just got a phone call from a very much alive Parker McCoy."

"That's impossible. Are you sure?" Ben asked.

"Dead sure. I've been on the phone non-stop, but no one I can pull favors with is in range to look into this. It has to be you five."

"All of us? Isn't that a little overkill, sir?" Rourke asked.

"You haven't heard the best part yet. Parker's being held captive by Deacon James and The Mortician."

"They killed him just so they could kidnap him and resurrect him later. What in the hell could they be planning," Rudyard said aloud.

"Shit," Arnold cursed. "It's the old days all over again."

"Sounds like a rescue mission. Where are we headed boss?" Rourke queried.

"Trace got me an address of an old dairy farm in Vermont. A little town, name of—" said.

"Brattleboro," Rudyard interrupted. "Oh dear. Deacon's gone home."

CHAPTER NINETEEN

Standing outside Rudyard Sinclair's tent, Rourke waited impatiently. Ben emerged from the tent behind him.

"We need to get moving," Ben said.

"I know. They ready yet?" His partner asked.

"Not yet."

"If this were anything other situation, I'd take the opportunity to just leave them here. But superhuman alien cannibals and folks that raise the dead are more than I can handle by myself," Rourke admitted.

"I mean, it isn't like you'd be completely alone anyway."

"True enough. Ben?"

"Hmmm?"

"When I put that thing around my neck, I saw Jill and she reminded me of something. I never... I never did apologize to you that day you came over after she died. I ran you off when you were just trying to help. I told you "Mind your own business, you fucking paddy," like you weren't Jill's best friend too. You were always there for us. I'm sorry, Ben. I've tried to make it up to you, but I'm no better than those dinosaurs in the tent behind us."

"It's fine, Rourke. I know it hurt. She was my friend too, and you...well, you've always been an asshole. At least you've been an asshole that's got my back."

Rourke smiled. "When this shit is over and done with, we'll go out like old times. Hit up some of the bars near the Mall. The sooner we can get this behind us, the better. I don't like it, and neither did Jill."

"Rourke, they're Exceptionals. I can't remember a time you ever did like them."

Rourke chuckled under his breath.

The flap of Rudyard's tent opened and Ben gasped. One by one the former superheroes, Rudyard, Troy, and Arnold stepped out into the sun. Troy and Arnold had shed their civilian clothes and were wearing their classic uniforms. Before them stood not Arnold Grant and Troy Berlin but The Crimson Howl and The Automatic Man. Rudyard, of course remained in his Swami disguise, looking much like the fortune teller he had become over the years.

Arnold's costume was cobbled together patch job. His crimson leggings had runners in places and there was a hole over his left kneecap. His crimson shirt, emblazoned with a black wolf's head, was tucked into the pants a size too tight and the belt he wore was practically busting. His gut hung over the belt precariously. He wore a mid-length red cape with patchy wolf fur at the shoulders. Instead of his classic wolf's head cowl, he was wearing a simple black masquerade mask. His gloves were black and ran up to his forearm. Each finger had a stainless-steel fingernail sewed into the fabric that looked sharp to the touch and aching for blood. Completing the look was a mid-length red cape.

Troy's outfit was much more put together. He too had a cheap party mask, but his was dark blue instead of black. His blue and silver jumpsuit was flawless, unmarred by holes or tears. Troy's cape was shorter than Arnold's, silver with a dark blue streak.

Rourke kept himself from rolling his eyes. Ben was transfixed, watching the three men with a sort of childlike awe with his mouth open.

"Wow," Ben whispered.

Rourke sighed. "Please don't say 'to the Howl Mobile', Arnold. I honestly don't think I can handle that right now."

To his surprise, the men smiled at him. "Kid, I know this probably looks ridiculous to you," Arnold stated the obvious.

"Taking everything I got to keep from laughing, not gonna lie," Rourke concurred.

Arnold chuckled. "But we got to talking, and if Parker McCoy is in trouble and in need of rescuin', well, we might as well do it right."

In a way, he respected their commitment. These costumes meant something to them and that had a value all its own. Who better to take on a mission against a zombie-making supervillain and an alien cannibal?

"Well then. To the Howl Mobile!"

Ben led the four men walked down the boardwalk towards Arnold's car. Rourke noticed that the people they passed stopped what they were doing and stared at them, mouths open, whispering to each other. Little kids tugged on their mom's pants and pointed. Teenagers looked at one another and snickered.

One of a pair of older guys, a thin fellow with a hat declaring that he had served in the Korean War let out a whoop, removed his cap, and waved it at them.

"Crimson Howl's back," he cheered.

"Give 'em Hell, Automatic Man," his companion shouted. He was sitting in a wheelchair and let out a mighty whistle.

"See, Irish," Arnold said, "there's people what still remember us. They may be old but they remember!" Arnold slapped Ben on the shoulder, careful not to scratch him with the claws on the gloves.

A flock of people of all ages came closer, most of them with their phones out, trying to get a picture. A man in his forties approached Troy and held out his hand. Troy reached out and shook it with a smile.

"My grandfather and great uncle were Exceptionals!" He declared proudly. "Do you remember Captain Quick and Citizen Sand?"

"Sure do!" Arnold answered. "They had a villain named the Jellyfish. Used to terrorize the G.I.'s at the Brooklyn Naval Yard if I recall correctly."

The man's eyes beamed. "That's right!" He pulled out his camera and asked to take a picture. "My great uncle is still alive. Nearly a hundred. I can't wait to tell him I saw you guys!"

"Just like the old days," Rudyard said to Rourke. "We used to not be able to walk down the street without people coming up to us in gratitude asking for an autograph or picture."

It was one of the most surreal sights either of the two agents had ever witnessed in their time at the Task Force. The crowd continued to press, asking for autographs and grabbing pictures. Troy waved at them, smiling broadly as they climbed into Arnold's car.

Arnold, now behind the wheel of his car, started the engine. It roared to life and the people cheered loudly. Arnold revved the engine to the delight of the people and drove off, tires screeching. Arnold honked the horn and gave a wave as they peeled off.

Inside, it was all smiles. Troy was grinning like a kid on Christmas. "Well, how about that!"

"They still remember," Rudyard marveled.

It was going to be a five-hour drive from Seaside Heights to Brattleboro but none of them seemed to mind the cramped car. As they sped down Highway 35 towards the Garden State Parkway, Rourke heard Jill's voice in the back of his head, warning him again. He shivered.

"Everything all right, Agent Harken?" Rudyard asked.

"I'm fine. Just excited. Getting to the bottom of this and all."

"Well, if you need to talk, let me know."

•••

The man who had first noticed the three superheroes pulled out his phone and made a call.

"They're on their way. Awaiting further instructions."

The voice on the other end said, "Go home. Get your costume. Wait for the signal."

The old man hung up and walked off to his car.

CHAPTER TWENTY

The heat of the afternoon always made Gabrielle Klien-Jurowicz uncomfortable. Her husband was the one who had insisted they move to Arizona, and he was dead. Saul hadn't left her with enough of a nest egg to move, but at least the pool was always cool and inviting.

Her phone rang. She rarely received calls. Her children were grown. Her son was a fishing boat captain and her daughter was a Marine Biologist. They hardly ever called, but that was all right. She didn't like to bother her children much. Gabrielle picked up the phone.

"Yes?"

"This is Director Hollis. All assets are being reactivated. Continue the phone chain." Then, dead air.

Gabrielle stood and crossed the house to her bedroom and changed into her old bathing suit, the one that looked like fish scales. She hadn't worn it in years.

Gabrielle stepped out onto the concrete patio and seethed as the dry Arizona heat wafted into her air-conditioned home as if she'd opened her oven door.

The water glistened cheerily, calling her as always. She stepped outside and dove into the deep end of the pool. Gabrielle swam to the bottom and sat there for twenty minutes before coming back up. The Mermaid smiled, her aged face now smooth and ravishing in the mid spring sun. The gills on the side of her neck opened and closed rapidly. She would have to get her trident back from Arnold Grant, that old slob, and that was okay too. She let out a laugh. It was going to be so good to be back.

•••

Roy Daubes was doing a quintuple life sentence. He didn't remember what exactly for. It was lonely in solitary confinement and it did funny things to his head. On his first day in prison in 1969, he had murdered three inmates. He had crushed one's skull with his bare hands, tore the larynx out of the next, and caved in the final inmate's chest with a kick. After that, they kept him alone in a dark box.

Once, he had been known as Mister Lucifer.

When he was thrown in jail by Deacon James and Troy Berlin, he felt strange. The urge to murder fell away after a couple weeks. Every day, he'd sit and stare at the wall, getting up only to take a piss or eat the food they served him. It was his only routine, never broken once in forty-seven years.

Until today.

The slot opened up and the guard passed an envelope through.

"Your parole letter, Mister Daubes," the guard said, his voice flat.

Roy opened the letter. There in black and white was his parole letter, signed by the governor and the warden both. He looked at the mold growing at the edges of the paper and sneered. They had let it sit long enough.

The steel door swung open, its creaking echoing through the hall. The guard stared straight ahead. As Roy stepped out and stretched, he felt the old itch come over him again. He looked and saw they were alone.

At shift change, the guards would find a dead body with its tongue torn out and an empty cell where Roy Daubes was supposed to be. There'd be no mention in the incident report that Mister Lucifer was out killing again.

•••

In a small church in Boston, Father Nathaniel Cunningham silently counted the donations from this morning's mass at his desk. He sighed. Fewer and fewer of his flock were showing up. Every year, it seemed a parishioner would die or convert or just stop coming and no one would replace them. He didn't blame them. He himself had had a crisis of faith years ago. When he found out that some of the priests he had known were sexually abusing altar boys and girls he had tried to talk to the Bishop, but was told it would be handled internally but nothing ever came of it.

When he found out the priests who had done such unspeakable acts to children were being transferred instead of being prosecuted something snapped in him. The priests begged for mercy when he visited them, dressed in black, a mask covering his face. Red marks on his hands and feet were the only color aside from the crown of thorns he wore on his head. He'd beaten the men with a cross made of wood; one he'd hand-carved himself.

Father Cunningham felt old now. He was managing his soup kitchen and the donation box was dwindling. Corruption was rising, faith was falling, and he was just an old priest. The rectory phone rang and he picked it up.

"Yes, Father Cunningham speaking."

"Father, this is The Mermaid. All assets are being reactivated. Continue the phone chain."

"Thank you, sister, for delivering me this miracle."

All Saints' Day was coming.

•••

Larry Ladeau received the letter in his cheap flophouse room in New Orleans. He wasn't sure how they found him, but he didn't care. It was an invitation back into the spotlight. So what if they had let the letter get a little dirty? He was so excited he'd get another crack at being The Mud Bug again; he almost pissed himself with excitement. Larry was nothing more than a small-time hood who barely made enough to live in the dingy boarding house. Lately, he had taken to going into foreclosed homes stripping them of the copper pipes, and selling them. The Mud Bug though? The Mud Bug demanded some respect.

He went to his closet and found his old costume, a brown pinstripe suit and hat, a mask with red whiskers, and his old revolver. Larry polished his pincer (pruning shears painted red and attached to a welding glove.)

He left the boarding house and tried to rob the First Financial Bank. There, he was shot twenty-eight times by New Orleans police, moldy letter still in his jacket pocket.

•••

As Director Hollis sat at his desk making phone calls, he received a text message from a contact of his at the postal service. All told, there were eighty letters that had been sent from Brattleboro, Vermont that matched his criteria. A file followed the message showing the addresses and delivery disposition. All eighty had been successfully delivered.

Hollis looked down at his call list and the eighty names his phone chain was trying to reach. It'd have to do. He grabbed his keys off his desk and ran out to his car. He hoped he wouldn't get there too late.

CHAPTER TWENTY-ONE

Arnold's Dodge roared its way up Route 95 North. The ride was filled with hurried discussion of strategy. They were heading to the old Cyrus King dairy farm across the road from Deacon's childhood home. Deacon was dangerous, that much was sure. How much more dangerous would he be in a place he knew?

"Rudyard, can your Medallion do anything to undo Deacon's mind control? I'm not excited about crawling around Deacon's turf where a loose bit of mold might turn any one of us on the others."

"It's possible," Rudyard admitted. "But if he infects me, I don't know if the Medallion would be strong enough to negate a direct attack. If he made me remove the Medallion before I could shake the mold's control, its power would be rendered useless."

"Are we sure it's even going to come down to some sort of brawl? This is Deacon we're talking about. The only people that ever had to get physical with him were criminal scum or inept law enforcement. We're his friends. That should count for something, shouldn't it," Troy asked.

"I hope so," Rourke answered. "This might be a throwback to the old days for you guys, but we're brand new to scrapping with open villains."

"That's been really bothering me too. How long has The Mortician been a part of this?" Ben asked.

"Everybody knows Roger Rapowski is just a scuzzy bum living in some flea-bitten trailer park in New Jersey," Arnold replied. "He was one of the first villains to hang up the costume."

"Arnold, I trust Director Hollis on this," Rudyard said. "You and Troy had plenty of foes of your own. I was the one who fought with The Mortician the most. There's a sadistic streak in that one. Whatever compelled him to retire, I have a feeling he's been waiting for this for some time. I've been putting out calls to the spirit world as you've been driving."

"Bullshit," Troy coughed.

Rudyard rolled his eyes and continued. "—and what I found was disturbing. He locked a man in a morgue freezer alive and left him there to die. I found the ghost of a child whose eyes were torn out by one of his monstrous creations. Whatever his reasons, he's just as brutal as he's ever been."

The car was quiet for moment before Arnold spoke. "Still don't add up. Why would Deacon go through the trouble of killing Parker then have The Mortician revive him?"

"To get all of you together so he can finish you off, that's why," Rourke deduced. "You've got enhanced senses. Can't you smell this is a trap?"

"Trap or not, we've got to save McCoy," Troy was adamant. "He's the one with enough brains to figure out how to stop Deacon from killing innocent people again. We..."

"Arnold, this is our turn," Rudyard interrupted.

Arnold spun the wheel and the Dodge veered onto Putney Road. The sun was beginning to sink low in the sky and the pastoral landscape and rolling hills were peaceful and inviting. Ben shuddered.

"You all right, buddy?" Rourke asked.

Ben gave him a half smile. "Fine. Just a little rattled. Trying to wrap my head around it all."

That Rourke could understand. "Get ready, I think we're here."

Cyrus King's now dead dairy farm had been abandoned for the past thirty years. Over-grown weeds and grass stood nearly thigh high and the old cow barn had been all but stripped of its red paint. Broken bits of what once was a sign marking the place as the old King Dairy lingered like old ghosts on the side. Holes of varying size checkered the roof and Ben was amazed it hadn't caved in after so many years and so many snows. A few hundred feet away lay the foundation of what he assumed was Deacon James' old house.

The Dodge stopped at what used to be the foot of the dirt driveway leading up to Deacon's house. Arnold killed the engine and for a moment there was a hush over them.

Arnold turned and looked at Rourke and Ben.

"You guys can sit this one out if ya' want to. This is between us and Deacon. Rourke, you're build decent enough to be good in a scrap, I'll give you that. Irish, you're just as smart as a whip. If you wanna lay low while we handle this, no one will fault ya for it."

Rourke grinned. It was the first time Arnold bothered using his name. "It's our job, Arnold. We were called in to this, we have to see it through." He looked at his colleague. "Right, Ben?"

Ben's voice cracked. "That's right."

"Then let's do this," Troy said and they emptied out of the car.

"I guess we're going to have to get into that barn. Ben and I will spread out and see if there's a back way," Rourke took charge.

"Don't be an idiot, kid,"Arnold snapped. "This ain't one of them cop shows. We're just gonna walk in."

"But what about the element of surprise?" Ben asked.

"Hard to get the drop on someone who is expecting you, Agent," Troy commented. "I can't imagine Parker McCoy's call went unnoticed after all this time."

Arnold motioned for them to follow him. The three costumed heroes went first, followed by Rourke and Ben who had unholstered their guns and kept them low. The men waded through thigh-high grass until they came to the front of the barn. The door, weather-beaten and nearly detached from the frame, fell off when Arnold moved it. It landed with a thud on the tall grass. The smell of rotten hay, wet wood, and mildew came from the inside.

In the waning daylight, there was very little visibility left. As they entered the barn, Rourke expected to see McCoy tied up to an old metal chair, a thick handkerchief tied around his mouth. Instead, there was nothing.

Rudyard touched The Medallion of Delphi and it began to glow brightly, illuminating the barn with a warm, white light. Rourke and Ben raised their guns at the man they saw standing in the corner of the barn.

"Don't shoot!"

They lowered their weapons. Rourke was shocked to recognize his boss. "Director Hollis?"

The GAT Director walked toward the light, a narrow-shouldered man with an easy smile, steel gray hair beginning to turn white, and a chubby face. He was dressed in an Armani suit. He too was carrying a gun. His badge was draped around his neck on a chain.

"Hello boys," he greeted. "Thought you could use the help. Came as fast as I could." He looked over at the superheroes. "Gentlemen, I hope you've treated my men well."

"Of course, Director," Troy swore.

"Good. I'll dispense with the pleasantries since we're in a heap of shit here. Swami, if you wouldn't mind illuminating that patch of ground over there, you'll see what I'm talking about."

Rudyard turned to his left and the light from the Medallion grew brighter until the entire barn was completely lit. Ben looked at the area Rudyard had illuminated. The ground was scorched as if it had been lit on fire leading to a large, circular hole in the ground. "What is it, sir?"

Hollis shook his head. "That is the world of shit we're in. If you'd fix your gaze upward you'll see we're just about an hour too late."

The men looked up and saw the hole in the old roof. Something had torn through it. "What on earth made that?" Ben asked.

"A rocket. Pretty impressive one. Carrying a payload engineered by The Mortician, Deacon, and Parker McCoy himself. Before you ask, I don't have any idea what exactly it is. We need to get below though, in a hurry."

"What are you talking about? What the hell is going on?" Rourke asked, then paused. "How did you get here before us anyway?"

"I flew," Hollis answered. "Private plane. Brattleboro has its own airfield. I think it would be best, boys, if you let him explain everything."

"What are you talking about, Mister Hollis?" Rourke barked. "Let who?"

Hollis sighed. "Dr. McCoy, of course. Come with me, gentlemen, it'll be much easier if you let me lead the way." Hollis walked over to the other side of the barn and pulled something from his pocket. Rourke thought it was a cell phone, but it was too small for that. Hollis tapped it with his thumb. The wall moved, sliding smoothly open to reveal a set of steel doors. The doors slid open.

"An elevator?" Rourke identified.

Hollis smiled. "Astute, Rourke. It's either take this one or the one in the hangar. Now come on. Dr. McCoy will be waiting."

"Isn't Deacon James with him?" Ben asked. "Shouldn't we make some sort of plan?"

"Oh yes, Ben. Deacon is with him. The Mortician left an hour or two ago. But I assure you he is the least of the problems we're having. We really want to come inside before the rocket gets much higher."

Ben looked at Rourke. "This doesn't feel right."

"To get cold feet now of all times? Still, at least you boys have good reflexes." Hollis shook his head. "But we really don't have time to lose."

"Let's go." It was Rudyard's voice now, but with none of the amiability it once had.

"Rudyard, what are you—" Rourke started to say but the world went black.

CHAPTER TWENTY-TWO

As Ben woke and took a breath, his nose filled with hospital smell. The harsh LED lights overhead were so bright they stung Ben's eyes when he opened them. He looked over and saw that Rourke was all right. He was sitting up and looking for his gun. Ben went for his but discovered it was missing.

"What happened? Were we drugged?" His voice echoed in the long room.

Rourke had a sour look. "We've been had."

"But we really don't have time to lose."

Ben gave him a puzzled look. The Agents came to their feet. "What do you mean?"

Rourke motioned to the far end of the room. It was bone white and sterile. Ben's face drained of color. Deacon James was sprawled on his back on the floor, a metal choker around his neck. He wore his work boots and the ragged whites from his days at the sanitarium. He was chained to a solitary steel beam that ran from floor to ceiling. His eyes glowed green and he struggled in vain with the metal band around his neck.

Rourke starting walking over to the shackled Deacon. Ben put his hand on his shoulder and stopped him.

"Don't. If he touched you... "

Rourke shrugged him off. "I know."

Ben looked around the room. The walls were smooth stainless steel, both a door and what Ben guessed was an elevator located behind them. He assumed they had been taken into the elevator and this was some underground bunker.

"You said we've been had," Ben reminded him. "By who?"

Rourke ignored him. "Where are they?" Rourke shouted at Deacon. "Why are we here?"

Deacon did not answer, only snarled at the choker and clawed at it furiously.

The door behind them slid open and Dr. Parker J. McCoy stood in the doorway. At first glance, he appeared to be at the pinnacle of good health, but Ben caught the faint smell of decay accompanying him.

"Good evening, gentlemen. I'm so very sorry we had to do it this way, but you really are too clever for your own good. I warned Hollis that you might hesitate." He approached them and held out his hand.

"I assure you, I'm not a zombie or a vampire. Honest."

Ben shook McCoy's hand. Rourke followed.

McCoy's smile widened. "I have to thank you, really I do. Your professionalism and commitment to your duties is remarkable. When all is said and done, I'm going to see to it you both get triple your current salaries."

Ben and Rourke exchanged wary looks. "How are you still alive, Doctor McCoy?" Ben asked. "We saw the hole in your abdomen. There was no way ..."

"Easy, Agent Mulcahey. I have friends in high and low places. The Mortician was more than happy to assist in my revival. Director Hollis, Warren, tells me you're just about the best subject matter expert he's ever seen."

"Where are the others?" Rourke queried. "And why is Deacon James chained up like that? Why is there a hole in the roof of this place?"

"They will be here shortly," McCoy informed them. "Rudyard told me to tell you both he was sorry for having to knock you out, but he was getting impatient." He walked past Rourke and Ben and went over to Deacon James.

"As for this little problem, the answer is simple. Once I was bought back from oblivion, I was able to subdue him. No easy task."

Deacon stopped what he was doing and turned his eerie green gaze to McCoy. He rolled over and tilted his head. Suddenly Deacon rocked back on his feet and lunged towards him, arms outstretched. Before Deacon could reach McCoy, he found the chain was too short, the choker too strong, and snapped backward, landing hard on his knees.

"Easy," McCoy chided. "You're frightening our guests."

The door slid open and Rudyard, Troy, Arnold, and Warren Hollis entered. They stood in silence off to the side. McCoy nodded. "Now that everyone is here, shall we begin?

"The world is changing, gentlemen." McCoy began. "There is about to be a significant shift in the way the world works in about fifteen minutes. An hour ago, I launched a rocket from this bunker with the assistance of The Mortician, a control room full of fine folks in Washington, and, albeit unwillingly, Deacon, here."

"What is it going to do?" Ben asked.

"Deacon James, at least the part of him that makes him interesting and useful, was kind enough to supply me with a great deal of his blood. You are aware of its hunger for human flesh, yes? And its ability to control peoples' minds? I decided to take advantage of my untimely demise and dear Deacon's condition, in order to finish something I started a long time ago. We're bringing back the Exceptional People's Act."

"What?" Ben reacted. "How?"

"Agent Mulcahey, you don't seriously believe that I came up with the Act out of sheer altruism, do you? I was able to gain a great deal pitting one side against the other, as I have always done. People are so ready to hand over their freedoms when salvation comes wrapped in spandex, patriotism, or the occult.

"Of course, short-sighted politicians have always been the problem. There should've been no further wars after World War II. We had demonstrated the capabilities of Exceptionals to succeed in military operations and at home. Instead, they decided to focus on Communism of all things. Vietnam was a public relations disaster, and years of work were undone."

"Years of work?" Rourke repeated. "Are you trying to tell me you organized World War II?"

"Well, yes. Poor economies are easy to exploit by racist fascists. I just had to use the correct proxies. America was no more difficult. Promise them superhuman soldiers and governments eventually open their pocketbooks. Then they forget who's in charge and run off into bloody combats in the jungle. Vietnam ruined the public's faith in heroes, and I had to improvise. Had to use my extensive reach to prove to the world it needed the Exceptionals. Hostages in Iran, a war in Afghanistan with the Soviets, crack in the inner cities... Hell, I ushered in the age of terrorism with airliners crashing into skyscrapers, airport bombings, and mass shootings but these Washington idiots still wouldn't budge on it."

"They never were particularly sharp, were they Parker?" Warren laughed.

McCoy shook his head. "No, Warren, they were not. Thankfully we got you in place to help fix that."

Rourke's mouth hung open. "You...,?"

"You ever hear of those conspiracy theories about a secret government controlling world events?" McCoy grinned. "Only half true. World events are controlled by me."

"Impossible," Ben fired back.

"Not really, Agent Mulcahey. Creating Exceptional heroes and villains is easy as well. Everyone longs for power. One man's hero is another's enemy. The Germans and Soviets were happy to volunteer subjects. By the time I was done with them, I could create my own. Dr. Newglory's remains stitched together with the failed soldiers from Troy's experiment created The Doctor. Once Deacon James sought me out, and I started studying the mind control spores, it became even easier to make villains on demand. Losing the Exceptional People's Act set me back, but I still had a network of contacts.

"You see, as the world's smartest man, I see things differently than other people. It's my Exceptional ability. Which leads me to this. Why we're all here several stories underground. You see, in, what, ten minutes now, as I said, will change." He motioned to Deacon. "I created a virus based on Deacon's alien friend. It should infect approximately a third of the planet. No one will know they are infected, of course. I figured out how to turn off the parasite's little deal-making consciousness but when people start killing and eating each other, that'll certainly make the news. With your little road trip being noticed by the media and a rash of villain attacks about to start, the Exceptionals will be welcomed back with open arms. The Act will have to be reinstated, won't it Warren?"

Warren Hollis towards Rourke and Ben. "Oh, there is no question of that. We've had our best lobbyists working tirelessly to convince the less sympathetic ones to our side. An outbreak of violent cannibalism linked back to some mad alien out of the cosmos, at the same time costumed villains come back? It's pretty much a done deal, fellas."

"You know about all this?" Rourke uttered in disbelief. "You're going to allow him to—"

Hollis put his hand on Rourke's shoulder, "Rourke, do you know who my mother is? These men here rescued her from being tortured to death in a cultist's den. Without McCoy's best guys, I wouldn't be here. I owe these men the chance to do what they're best at."

"At the expense of the entire world?" Ben shouted. "This is insane!"

"Any more insane than what's going on now, Ben? Any crazier than a man wearing a Medallion that actually shows him the other side and other dimensions? A genetically modified human who will kill on command? An alien living inside a man who previously had the I.Q. of dirt? People need men like these. Not to give them hope but to keep them in line. Keep them coddled so their betters can improve the world without their interference."

"Their betters?" Rourke spat. "You've been blowing people up so they'll let your friends play dress-up when you could have been curing cancer?"

"That would be giving away too much, Rourke. Every crisis is a gift. Once the world is compliant, then the big changes can happen. This may seem like a bit much, and I know you miss your wife, but this doesn't have to be so dramatic. It isn't like you're the only one who's made sacrifices," McCoy remarked.

Rudyard rolled his eyes. "Mine didn't have anything to do with you, Parker. Anthony died instead of me in order to satisfy The Medallion."

"But it was a sacrifice," Parker McCoy continued. "Arnold gave up Lady Panther to her own people as a bargaining tool. It was hard for him, but he made the right choice. Troy's kept faithful to Vera even though he's been well aware I surgically altered her to be compliant to him in all things. He's been a model American lad, upstanding and patriotic. It can be even easier for you two boys."

Warren Hollis agreed. "It's true. I made sure that you'd at least be offered a seat at the table."

Ben's eyes narrowed. "What do you mean?"

"When the Act is reinstated our outfit is going to expand. I'll more than likely get a cabinet post. Ben, you're going to be my successor. Rourke, you get a cushy position training new recruits in fieldwork. We're going to triple what you currently make. All we ask is that you keep this quiet. We're so far down that when the virus is released, we won't be affected by it. I made sure of that."

"And if we refuse?" Ben dared to ask.

"That would be... unfortunate," McCoy responded. "We're prepared to deal with that, if need be."

"We're just supposed to go along with it all? You're set to kill billions of people just to create a threat large enough justify a police state run by Exceptionals?"

"Kid, it's a lot more complicated than it looks," Arnold said.

"This is what we do, fellas" Troy added. "So, if a few people gotta die so the rest of us can make a comeback to do what we do best, we gotta take that chance. What's a few lives with the ability to fix the whole world at stake."

"You've seen it Rourke, only you know out of all of them, just what the Medallion of Delphi truly is. It can't go to waste telling fortunes for fat housewives on the boardwalk. It was meant for so much more," Rudyard pleaded.

"The deal McCoy is offering, boys, is lucrative. It benefits everyone, really," Hollis reminded them.

Ben frowned. "And all we have to do is sit here and wait for it to happen."

"It's not like you could stop it, Ben. Even if you wanted to its too late. In less than five minutes, the rocket will disperse the virus. People will be infected."

"And then the killing starts? Everyone from here to Timbuktu starts tearing each other apart?" Rourke verbilized. "When Ben first dragged me on this trip, I was laughing about what a bunch of washed up old hacks you all were, how you were fake as pro wrestling and twice as cheesy. I remember laughing at Ben, saying that if your McCoy was so goddamn smart he could cure cancer, why hadn't he already?"

He continued, looking at each of them with contempt. "You guys realize this is insane right? For all the sleazy racist shit you throw around Arnold, you've been upfront about being heroes the entire time. Same goes for you, Troy. Your sense of justice might be royally fucked up, but you've been about helping people. Especially you Rudyard." He motioned to McCoy. "This guy isn't a genius. He's crazy. McCoy here wants to murder the world and you're okay with it as long as you get to put the uniform back on?" He turned to his boss. "Mister Hollis, surely you have more sense than this."

Hollis looked offended. "We've been planning this in secret for years, Rourke. We knew Deacon would come for McCoy someday. McCoy's been taking a serum for the last ten years that makes his bodily fluids a sedative for Deacon. Deacon took a bite out of him sure, and fell asleep like he ate a Thanksgiving turkey. When he did, I moved in, secured Deacon, and activated McCoy's alarm. With you two on the case and keeping law enforcement distracted, I reactivated The Mortician with a dose of mold. He acquired McCoy's body for us, repaired him as best we could, and brought him back to life for us. Everything is going as planned, Rourke. No one here is crazy, except you if you turn down this offer."

Rourke laughed crazily. He pointed at the three old heroes, then at Parker McCoy. Ben watched the rage building in McCoy's face as Rourke guffawed. Arnold started toward him.

"I told you when this was over, you and me were gonna tussle," Arnold swung at him. Rourke ducked under Arnold's swing and drove his right fist into Arnold's stomach. Arnold grunted and grabbed Rourke by the hair with his right hand. He lifted Rourke off the ground. "Yeah, you coulda' been good in a scrap. Now be a good boy and say hi to Badger for me."

With his left hand, Arnold flexed his costume's claws and slashed Rourke's throat. A fountain of red sprayed from the agent's neck. Arnold dropped to the floor. Rourke crawled across the floor towards Ben, only making it a few feet. The spurting blood turned into a dribble, pooling at Ben's feet. He gazed up at Ben.

"Jillian was right," he gurgled, laughed once last time, then went limp. What was left of the life of Rourke Harken was just a puddle of blood, the color of the Crimson Howl's cape, staining the pristine white floor.

Before Ben could react, Troy was behind him, locking his arms together.

"I don't want to hurt you, kid," Troy hissed, "but try anything and you'll never jerk off with these hands again."

Ben was too stunned to speak or struggle. It was over in a matter of seconds. The final laugh on Rourke's face never fading, mocking everyone around him as his body seized.

John Rourke Harken was dead.

Ben screamed.

CHAPTER TWENTY-THREE

"Well, looks like Rourke's out. What about you Ben? Are you going to be a team player?"

Those were the last words Ben heard before he had blacked out. He awoke on the cold white floor, a chain around his neck like Deacon had worn. He blinked his eyes and lifted his head to look around. He was in the same lab before, but now he was in Deacon's place, chained to the steel beam.

Rourke's body still lay in the middle of the room. Ben jerked angrily at the chain, straining to reach his friend. The elevator door across the room slid open and McCoy entered holding a leash. Deacon trailed behind him, walking obediently.

"You're awake. That's good," McCoy said. "You passed out before answering Warren last night. Would you do me the favor of answering that question now? Will you join us?"

Ben spat at McCoy.

"I expected as much. You are certainly the sharper of the two. That's why you didn't waste your life on theatrics. But I can see this will take some convincing. First, you should know that the dispersal seems to have gone off perfectly. A few rogue reports of people going wild are appearing in the news. That will accelerate nicely. Also, there's been a murder spree in southeast Missouri. Crazy, right? Matches Mister Lucifer's old M.O." Parker smiled. "Oh Deacon? It's breakfast. You may have Rourke's left hand. Enjoy."

Deacon dropped to all fours and bounded to Rourke's corpse. He lifted Rourke's left arm, sniffing, before taking Rourke's ring finger in his mouth. With a sickening crunch, he dug in his teeth. There was a wet tearing sound as Deacon stripped the flesh from Rourke's finger and swallowed it happily.

"Let him go, you monster! Put him down!" Ben screamed.

McCoy crouched in front of Ben. "Don't worry. In a couple days, there won't be much left of him. Deacon is very obedient when he's had his shots. But you! You're a different situation. You're smart enough to run the agency while Warren and I are busy elsewhere. That's why I need you. Rourke makes a fine martyr, but I would rather have you alive as a functionary."

"Fuck you!"

"I can appreciate that. But can you appreciate how difficult it is going to be keeping friends and family safe in this new world? You must be scared to death for your parents right now."

Ben's mouth hung open but he couldn't manage the words, just angry guttural noises.

"Exactly! If one of those nasties out there finds them, that would be just awful. You should really consider out offer." The sound of wet ripping and tearing subsided. "Deacon must be done. Hands aren't that filling."

Turning to look over his shoulder, McCoy shouted. "Go ahead and have his left foot as well. He's not going dancing anytime soon."

Ben wailed and slammed against the chains, his skin chafing and tearing under the metal collar.

"Sounds like you have some thinking to do my friend. You'll get there eventually. Everyone does," McCoy stood.

Once Deacon had finished peeling the meat from Rourke's foot, McCoy whistled. "Come on Deacon, we have work to do." Deacon stood and followed McCoy. As Ben watched them go, he saw Deacon turn. Their eyes met and Deacon stopped for just a moment. He nodded at Ben, then just as quickly, spasmed, and fell in line behind McCoy again.

Ben collapsed on the ground, crying for his dead friend and for himself.

•••

The next day, when Ben woke, both Hollis and McCoy were standing there with Deacon between them.

"Good morning! Glad you're awake. It's time for breakfast," McCoy said.

Ben's stomach rumbled.

Warren and McCoy both laughed. "Oh dear, are you hungry too? Well, let me see if there are any leftovers first, then. Deacon, fetch me Rourke's heart."

Deacon dropped from his standing position to all fours and pounced on Rourke's corpse, rolling it over. He ripped open Rourke's shirt and pushed his fingers into Rourke's chest. The bone cracked as Deacon dug in his fingers. He tensed his arms to pull.

"Make a wish," Hollis said.

Deacon ripped open Rourke's ribcage from the middle and reached in, wrapping a hand around Rourke's heart. He pulled it out with a wet rip. Deacon stood and walked to McCoy.

"Good work Deacon. That's yours to eat."

Ben crouched on the floor, watching Hollis and McCoy. Let them come closer, Ben thought, just a little closer. Let them relax too much.

"Watching Deacon eat Rourke's heart, I start to wonder about the people Rourke loved. I know you're worried about your parents, but I wonder who's looking after his parents? After Jill's? You know, I really hope none of these cannibals thinks to start digging up graveyards for the bones. It'd be a shame if Jill's grave was disturbed."

Ben lunged for them. "You fucking monsters!"

McCoy slapped Ben to the ground. "Cut the theatrics. You're a bookworm, not a fighter. You do this, and you live a long, happy life and so does the rest of your family. Deacon, clean yourself and this blood up. Lick it off the ground if you have to."

Ben lay on the ground, shaking in rage. Hollis bent down next to him. "Come on Ben, if we didn't need you, we'd have just killed you already. Just play ball. You get to be one of the heroes for a change, just like you always wanted."

Ben looked at Hollis, then Deacon. Deacon lapped at the blood on the floor eagerly. For a moment, he saw Deacon jerk his head up, his eyes no longer that bright alien green. His eyes met Ben's and his mouth made silent words.

"Deacon sorry."

Then, his eyes were green again, and he resumed drinking Rourke's blood from the floor. Ben pushed himself up shakily, eyes locked on Deacon.

"Let me get this right. I agree to fall in line, and I don't have to worry about anybody I care about ending up like... that?" Ben pointed at Rourke's corpse.

McCoy nodded. "Yes, that's right."

"Director Hollis gets a cabinet position because I'm assuming the president understands our situation. I become head of the G.A.T.F., train the new agents, and make sure that we keep everything running smoothly, and people in place where we need them."

"You're getting it," Hollis said.

"Two conditions, and they're non-negotiable since you already said you needed me."

McCoy laughed. "Go on."

"First, Rourke died a hero. I have no idea whether you're planning to stay dead after this, Mccoy, so I don't care who he's a hero for saving. But Rourke died a hero. Needs a plaque and everything at G.A.T.F. headquarters."

"Fine," was McCoy's answer.

"And second," Ben at Deacon. "That motherfucker gets put in the highest security box you can find and stays there until he rots."

Hollis reached out a hand to Ben. "Then, welcome aboard."

Ben took his hand and smiled.

EPILOGUE

The Exceptional People's Act was reinstated a full six months after Rourke died. Ben was at the ceremony when the President of the United States signed the bill back into law. It was met with a great deal of fanfare, heralded as a solution to the epidemic sweeping the country. Ordinary people were turning violent, hungry for human flesh. Old villains had reemerged as well, carving out a new bloody place for themselves. The President's own daughter was nearly the victim of a cannibal attack, but the Crimson Howl arrived just in time to save her, cinching the Act's approval.

Warren Hollis was indeed given a cabinet post and would oversee the expanded Golden Age Task Force, now called the Division of Exceptional Affairs. Parker McCoy was not present. He was still presumed dead and wanted it that way. Ben was cleaned up and sent back to Washington D.C. to oversee the expansion. He was moved out of the J. Edgar Hoover building and to a larger office near the Pentagon. He was made supervisor over fifty people, including field officers. Several of them were in training to become government funded heroes themselves as a part of Operation Golden. The Crimson Howl, The Automatic Man, and The Swami, were at the personal beck and call Parker McCoy. As no one questioned their actions, so they were the perfect catspaws.

Rourke's plaque hung in Ben's new office. Ben would use it to lecture new recruits on the selflessness of a good agent; how even among the greatest of heroes, it was John Rourke Harken who had rescued Director Hollis at the cost of his own life. It was because of him that Deacon James was locked in a lab beneath the Pentagon being studied for a cure. Rourke's funeral had been beautiful. Ben gave a eulogy that he no longer remembered and then they lowered what was left of Rourke into the ground next to Jillian.

The nightmares had come every night since.

Ben knew they would. They were his reminder to kill the sons of bitches. Every last one. From the moment he saw the human in Deacon James, he knew there was a way. It was time to plan, to think, to scheme, to play the role. There would be time for blood soon, and he would tear the whole system down and burn the wreckage.

•••

It was a miserable January morning when there was a knock at Ben's office door. "Come in," he called. The door swung open and in walked Arnold, Troy, and Rudyard.

Ben clapped his hands together. "What a pleasure! Please, sit, no need for America's finest to stand. Crimson Howl, would you close that door. Perfect. Thank you. What can The Division do for you?"

"Drop the act, Irish," Arnold grunted.

"No act. Parker's orders. What do you need?" Ben's excitement was gone from his voice.

"Parker didn't send us," Rudyard said. "We're here about Deacon."

Ben raised an eyebrow. "What about him?"

"How long are you three planning to keep him locked away? Parker has serum that can keep him in line," Rudyard asked.

"How long?" Ben responded. "How long? Forever. He's a trophy now, boys. Deacon gets to have his fluids extracted whenever McCoy needs some more for his experiments. Otherwise? He's just a monster in a box."

"You're just holding Rourke's death against him!" Arnold charged. "It isn't Deacon's fault that you rolled over like a gutless coward. He's an asset to this country."

"He is an asset! He's your most well-remembered victory. I mean, we lost Parker J. McCoy to him, and had an agent die in the line of duty because you three were rusty and couldn't stop your former friend from unleashing hell on a global scale... Still, it's your legacy boys. Embrace it."

Arnold stomped to the desk, slamming his fists against it. "You think you're bein' funny, Irish? I'll tell McCoy about this and you'll be—"

"I'll be what, Arnold?" Ben interrupted. "I'll be killed? Tortured? Fed to monsters? That's old news. I took the offer, I run The Division smoother than even Warren ever could, and I keep my paperwork in order. What about you?

Getting scared of the bitey bastards outside? Busting heads not as fun as it used to be? Is that why you're crying for your friend to be let out? So he can cover your asses?"

"Fuck you, Irish!" Arnold roared.

Rudyard put a hand on Arnold's shoulder. "Let me. Look Ben, I'm sure you're aware that it is getting worse out there. I don't know what Parker's plan is, but we could use Deacon's help."

Ben steepled his fingers in thought. "I see. Well, then let me say this. Fuck. Off. And I mean that. Every one of us in this room traded our souls for money, power, fame, or some combination therein. It wasn't ever going to last. So you go get McCoy's approval, or you get me a directive from Warren Hollis, and Deacon James will be a free man tomorrow. Until then, he stays put."

Rudyard backed away from the desk, confused. "Ben, you're smarter than this. Everyone could die if we don't get the support we need. Deacon might be our best weapon against them."

"Then if you die before me, make sure to save me a seat in Hell. Now get the fuck out of my office," Ben ordered.

Rudyard turned and headed for the door. Arnold stomped away; his fists clenched at his side. Troy stood silently at the back of the room. "What about you, Troy? No going haywire on account of my bad language?"

"No sir. You're higher on the food chain than me now, and I can't argue with superior officers, let alone strike them. No matter how badly I want to." He turned and followed Arnold and Rudyard out the door.

Hollis and McCoy would hear about this, no doubt. That was perfect. He was the obedient cog in the machine. It was almost time.

•••

Deacon's escape attempt one month later was explosive, brutal, and lasted all of three minutes.

The pressurized chamber McCoy had developed for him lost power for thirty seconds as electricians working the floor above disconnected the wrong conduit. With the power cut and seal disabled, Deacon burst free from his cell into the laboratory surrounding him. He grabbed the first two scientists closest to him and tore out their throats with his teeth.

The guards stationed at the lab entrance spun and fired. Their darts sank into his back before crackling with electricity. Deacon screamed and fell to the floor, every dart like a cattle prod, short-circuiting his nervous system. One of the guards put a foot on Deacon's neck to hold him down, while the other jabbed a needle into his neck.

As fast as he had gotten out, he was asleep again. Ben smiled and exited out of his surveillance camera program. It was time to contact Warren Hollis.

•••

Ben sat at home, pouring two shots of Tequila. It had been a long day. After thirty days of deliberation, the order came down from McCoy. Deacon was to be incinerated. There would be no more risk of a variable of his scale being on the loose. Warren assigned Ben to handle it personally. They couldn't trust the others to follow through.

Ben downed the first shot. It burned going down, unlike the body he threw in the furnace. Who would've thought it'd be down for maintenance?

Ben pushed the second shot across the table. Deacon reached out slowly, picked it up, and drank it. "Good monster," Ben said.

"Deacon is no monster," Deacon intoned.

"Right. Well, you'll have to prove it first. You responded pretty nicely to a dose of McCoy's obedience serum when I pulled you out of the waste chute. And with the lab analysis showing that your alien friend has a weakness to alcohol, I think we have a winning combination to keep human you towards the surface."

"Deacon will prove to you," Deacon set down the shot glass.

"I'm sure you will. You realize McCoy is afraid of you by now, yes? Just because you fell into his trap doesn't mean he's happy about you being able to kill him."

Deacon leaned forward. "Deacon is aware. Deacon left mark on McCoy long time ago. Deacon will find him and stop him."

Ben smiled. "I like your enthusiasm, but first things first. We need to pay my boss a visit."

So, on that rainy night in February, Ben Mulcahey and Deacon James began the dirty business of revenge, but not before stopping at Jillian Lane-Harken's grave one more time. Ben said a prayer kissed her headstone and made his way to Warren Hollis' apartment.

•••

The apartment door opened slowly. "Ben?" Hollis asked. "What is it? Can't it wait until morning?"

"I'm afraid not sir. There's terrible news."

"What news?"

"You committed suicide tonight and left a great deal of evidence behind. Let me come in so we can discuss further."

Warren's eyes doubled as Deacon pushed past Ben and grabbed Warren by the shoulder. Warren's eyes turned glossy, and his breathing slowed. "Yes," Warren mumbled, "please come inside."

"Such warmth and hospitality, wouldn't you say Deacon? Now, let's start with where our friend Parker J. McCoy is these days."

•••

THE WORLD WILL KNOW was written in Warren Hollis' blood. It was smeared on every wall, mirror, and cabinet in his own penthouse suite. His body swung from the ceiling fan above the dining room table, his slits wrists dripping onto the white tablecloth below. At the end of the table was a handwritten confession to the murder of Golden Age Task Force agent John Rourke Harken. It also stated that Warren Hollis was complicit in a vast conspiracy that implicated two dozen senators, fifteen congressmen, thirteen state governors, the President of the United States, Parker J. McCoy, Arnold Grant, Troy Berlin, and Rudyard Sinclair.

The public demanded answers and arrests. How much did the politicians know? Was it true? Had they caused the plague that had turned half the country into flesh-crazed killers? They were cutting checks with the taxpayer's money to both heroes and villains? The home of Benjamin Mulcahey was one of the first to be raided. When they broke down the door, they found it in shambles. The furniture had been smashed to pieces, paintings torn off the wall, laptop destroyed. A safe hidden behind a bookshelf had been ripped out of the wall and lay embedded in the floor, open and empty. The papers reported the Division head missing and begged for clues.

As the months rolled on, and the prison sentences were handed out, of the politicians, only the President escaped jail time. That was only because of a timely resignation and the Vice President pardoning him, upon taking the office. The Exceptional Peoples' Act remained intact as there was no other option now. The plague was worsening daily. They couldn't afford to lose the Exceptionals now. Vigilantes would still be able to operate with impunity.

Ben smiled as he read the news at a truck stop in Portland, Oregon. It was a small victory, but a victory nonetheless. He crossed Hollis' name off his list. He finished his cup of coffee and paid the waitress for the two meals. A very rare steak for Deacon and a plate of eggs for himself. Over the past few months, he had sort of grown attached to the man with the odd stare who called him by his first and last name but had added the word "friend" to his name.

"Let's go," Ben said and the two of them walked out of the truck stop unconcerned. Behind them the patrons continued eating and working, the gloss over their eyes your only clue something was amiss. They climbed into Ben's car, a blue Dodge Avenger.

"Where do we go next, Friend Benjamin Mulcahey?" Deacon asked in his monotone. Ben had been working with him on his speech patterns, but it was nearly impossible. "This town of Portland has proven fruitless in our search for Parker McCoy, the hated man, even though Deacon can feel that he is near."

"We're close Deacon, that's all that matters. Him next, then the others.

Ben looked at his face in the rearview mirror. He'd grown a beard which he'd have to shave one of these days. His eyes had bags under them, but the nightmares had stopped after the nasty business with Warren Hollis. He'd lost considerable weight on the road chasing leads that often proved for naught. He pulled his list from his pocket. One down, Rourke. One down and four more to go, old friend. I won't let you down. Not this time.

Not again.

THE END

ABOUT OUR CREATORS

THE WRITERS

PAUL LANDRI—Born in Brooklyn, New York and raised in Atlantic Highlands, New Jersey, Paul Landri resides in the Atlanta area with his wife Kathryn and their menagerie of pets where he writes and does freelance voice acting, of which he has won best-acting awards. Paul has been writing since he was ten years old. Paul teamed up with Jason Clark after a raucous meeting through a mutual friend. The two have been writing together since 2010 and are currently working on projects for the Atlanta Radio Theater Company (Check them out at www.ARTC.org) bringing to life vintage superheroes from the Golden Age of Comic Books called the Golden Age Action Hour and a Samurai adventure called The Seven Zombie Hunters.

The Crimson Howl Returns was started in late 2015 at a coffee house in Brattleboro, Vermont and completed three years and many edits later in an apartment in Las Vegas in 2018. Two sequels are currently in the works.

Follow Paul on Twitter for the latest Crimson Howl news and other projects he and Jason have in store for you! @Paul_Landri

JASON CLARK — grew up in rural Michigan, surrounded by equal parts forest and farmland, where he still currently lives with his wife and son. Jason has been writing and acting since a young age, and endeavors to share the gift of story-telling via role-playing games with his friends and family.

Jason met Paul at a long-time friend's wedding and became fast friends. They've been working together for over twelve years now, and currently partner on writing and performing radio plays with the Atlanta Radio Theater Company, with a special interest in shining a light on vintage story-telling with the Golden Age Action Hour and Seven Zombie Hunters radio shows in the works.

INTERIOR ILLUSTRATOR

SAM A. SALAS — has been an artist since the 70's. His first love has always been comics and comic book art. His greatest aspiration was to become a comic book artist with one of the major companies. In the mid 90's Sam and a small band of friends decided to publish his own comics. Thus was born ZUB

COMICS. The company published two titles. One was GREAT GALAX-IES! A science fiction anthology featuring all original stories with art by Sam. The other title was TELLURIA a fantasy title. In all, the company published 11 books and folded in the early 2000's.

Since then, Sam has done various freelance projects for local independent publishers including several stories for a book titled WICKED AWESOME TALES, and a few stories for Ron Fortier. Now mostly retired, he is always ready to take on new projects and looks forward to working with his friend Ron on this new book.

COVER ARTIST

TED HAMMOND — is a Canadian artist who has been creating amazing art for over twenty years. His work has appeared in magazines, ads, books and graphic novels just to name a few. Go to (www.tedhammond.com) to contact him and check out more of his work!

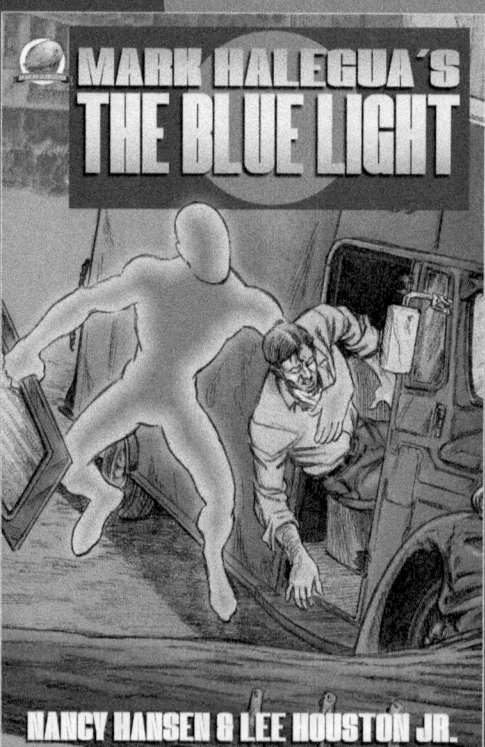